TILL DEATH SUE US PART

PERSEPHONE PRINGLE COZY MYSTERIES: EIGHT

PATTI LARSEN

CHAPTER ONE

Strains of Christmas music filled the car, the girls insisting we listen to carols on our drive up the mountain to the ski lodge not my first choice, but acceptable considering their giggling and warbling along. While I might not have been a huge fan of the classics, seeing my daughter, Calliope and her girlfriend, Thalia Vesterville, so happy and in love made the endless rounds of *Frosty the Snowman* and *Santa Claus is Coming to Town* worth it.

Mostly.

Since Thalia's rescue from the horrible recovery center where she'd been not only inhibited from healing but framed for murder, she'd bounced back from her surgery with the expected elasticity of the young, despite how dire things had been. When she

1

and Callie chose to live with me instead of returning to the ominous pile of rocks that was Thalia's ancestral home, I'd been delighted to see her shift almost immediately from desolate and despairing melancholy to the bright and lively young woman I always adored.

The fact she'd then closed up Vesterville House for the foreseeable future seemed another step in the right direction. Which made me think of her Uncle Gaines and the fact I hadn't heard a word from him since I'd messaged him about Thalia's recovery. And while being an international spy and assassin was likely taking up all of his time, I'd written him off as any kind of support to Thalia and did my best to banish him from my mind.

Gaines would, as always, do Gaines. All I could do was my best to protect Thalia from his influence if he ever did show his face again. Secret Agent Man or not, he'd better watch out when that happened, because he'd be getting a piece of my mind right before a swift kick in the posterior told him to get lost.

Talk big, don't I? Snort.

"How are the renovations going, you two?" I hadn't asked many questions about their newly purchased brownstone in downtown Wallace, their front door now within walking distance of every amenity and whatever fun there was to be had in our small town. My initial worry they'd uproot entirely and move to Portland or (gasp) out of state was assuaged when they'd bounced into my kitchen two weeks ago with the real estate listing for the property in hand and Thalia's remarkable inheritance ensuring a quick sale.

"It's going to take months," Callie groaned while her girlfriend laughed, hands stroking the soft, white fur of my therapy cat, Belladonna. The Christmas holidays meant no babysitter which in turn meant I had to take the bratty furchild with me. Not that I minded, and the white fluffmuffin herself seemed contented enough now that Thalia had freed her from the confines of her padded carrier. Still, Bella's penchant for sneaking out and scaring the willies out of me had me nervous about relocating her so far away, even for the weekend it was going to take to make sure Trent got married.

Oiy. Give me a minute. I'll get to that.

"We'll be off exploring the world while the workmen take care of everything," Thalia said in her new, breezy way of being, not a care on her face. "Lloyd will project manage for me," nice to know Lloyd Mitchem, retired special forces and family butler wasn't getting a pink slip, "and Sandra promised me she'd see to the greenhouse." The talented horticulturist, Sandra Lin, whose ongoing show *Plants That Kill* had given her enough fame she seemed delighted owed her position to Thalia, but I was still surprised Sandra could make time for such a job.

"It's going to be so cool, Mom," Callie said, now gushing too, round cheeks pink, a few wispy curls escaping her ponytail, hazel eyes full of excitement. "Lia's having a whole greenspace built on the roof. Garden, greenhouse, pond, all of it." I couldn't wait to see it, knowing the cost of such engineering would be staggering to someone like me, but a drop in the Vesterville bucket of wealth.

"That way I can still have my plants," Thalia said with a dreamy smile. The pair were such a contrast, the young heiress's thin, blonde hair barely enough to stay in her own ponytail holder, icy blue eyes huge in her lean face. Taller and built like a willow compared to my shorter, stocky daughter, they might have been opposites physically, but their absolute love and adoration for one another was the same.

"I'm excited to see it," I said as I slowed a little, winding up the switchback, a skiff of snow lacing its way across the black asphalt, brisk breeze in the valley turning to a stiffer wind that pushed the car a little.

"Anytime, Seph." Thalia leaned forward to Bella's irritation, one hand squeezing my shoulder. Any feelings I had of being their chauffeur went away, because of course they wanted to sit together and with Bella's carrier strapped in the front, it made sense. I realized I'd been holding that bit of resentment and let it go, the four-hour drive's tension mostly wiped away with that touch. Callie and I had head-butted frequently since she'd moved in with Thalia over personal space, privacy and minding my own business. The fact my daughter beamed her own smile at Thalia's offer told me maybe my kid had eased up on her need for such independence. Surely her girlfriend's recovery of health and their own relationship renewal had something to do with it. Peace of mind was a powerful balm. And maybe she was learning to trust that I only wanted her happiness.

Wait, I said most of my tension was gone, right? And didn't I mention something of the matrimonial bent that perked your ears? I'm getting to it.

"We really appreciate you coming with us," Thalia went on, sitting back again, Belladonna settling once more, purr firing up when the young woman returned her attentions to the cat. "It can't be easy."

Since these two really were the only reason I'd come at all, it was nice of Thalia to say so. "I'm delighted," I said, not really meaning it, though the end result was going to make me very happy, thank you. "This way I get to ensure your father actually goes through with it." I meant that as a joke, and Callie took it that way, thankfully.

"I don't think you have to worry," she said with a grin. "He's pretty excited. And I think he's happy you're coming."

"I'll stay out of the way as much as possible," I said. "I'm sure Melanie has everything planned to the detail." Part of me regretted saying yes, but not because I was driving up the mountain on Christmas Eve to be witness to my ex-husband's wedding the next night. No, I'd grown fond of spending Christmas alone, to be honest, choosing to spend that day hibernating, reading, drinking gin and eating the most decadent of foods while ignoring the world. Since even Mom and her husband, Ralph, had gone on a cruise this year for the holidays, that meant I didn't even have my own mother to have to worry about. Better yet? This year, I had the possibility of a special visitor, though any plans with the tall, dark and handsomely delicious Detective Kellan Boone were now up in the air. Thinking about Boone gave me shivers in the nicest way possible and I found myself grinning privately as Callie replied.

"Sounds like it." Callie said. "But I think it's pretty low-key."

That worked for me. While Boone and I had been on two lovely dates, we were both so busy in the few weeks since we'd met that carving out time to be together had proven a challenge. Still, the fact he'd made an effort on both occasions—beautiful restaurants, full attention, amazing kisses to wrap up both nights—gave me hope maybe we could find a way to make us work. And while I felt like I still knew so little about the Oregon-born, divorced and childless man I was quickly falling for, neither of us seemed in a huge hurry and I found I enjoyed learning new things about him over time, rather than having him dump his whole life in my lap. Considering what I did for a living, it was nice to just talk without an agenda.

Oh, and did I mention the kissing? The man could *kiss*. Yum.

My only concern that lingered like an old, sore tooth was the fact he hadn't yet replied to my half-joking (but not really joking) suggestion he meet me at the ski lodge after the wedding. I knew it sometimes took him a day or two to get back to me because of work, but I was honestly on pins-and-needles, concerned I'd moved too fast while doing

6

my best to reassure myself otherwise.

The thought of Boone in a hot tub had me squirming in my seat.

Callie's phone chimed and the moment she checked it she prodded Thalia. "Layla is already there, wondering where we are."

That was one giant redeeming factor, frankly. My dear friend—and Trent's—Sheriff Cherise King and her family were attending, naturally, which meant some late-night gin giggles with one of my closest friends. I relaxed further into the last few minutes of the drive, smiling out the windshield and finally kind of looking forward to the trip.

It was going to be a very Merry Christmas, I could just tell.

Oh, Seph. You had to say it.

CHAPTER TWO

I pulled up into the circular drive outside the lodge, parking as the girls piled out in a rush, Callie's bright red puffy ski jacket doing nothing to blend in like Thalia's pure white one. Thalia pulled open the passenger door as I got out, tucking Belladonna into her carrier with a soft, "there you go, sweet girl," while my cat immediately started muttering in protest.

To my surprise, Brin Anderson bounded out the front doors and threw herself into Callie's arms, the pair laughing and hugging before Brin did the same for Thalia. Trent's soon-to-be stepdaughter had traded her green-dyed semi-Goth look for something a bit more natural, though she still had purple streaks in her dark hair that caught the early

8

afternoon sunlight. When her hazel eyes met mine, the colored contacts were missing, as was the striking black liner, her facial piercings removed, and her slim body dressed in more conformist clothing that matched the girls. But the little gap remained between her front teeth giving her an even more endearing smile that made her look like a kid, not a young woman.

"Hi, Seph." She hugged me a bit breathlessly, smiling so wide I couldn't stop my own despite Belladonna's growing complaints. "Oh, Bella!" Brin rushed to take the carrier from me while a porter lifted our luggage from the trunk and loaded it on a trolly, the valet taking my keys and then my SUV when his companion was done with our things. While our first meeting had been rocky, Brin had visited the house enough over the last few weeks I'd come to adore her and she to trust me, or so it seemed. As for Melanie, Trent's fiancé no longer seemed to be terrified of me every time we encountered one another, much more relaxed since she and Trent decided to get married. The last time I'd seen her, she'd been smiling and happy and treated me with calm deliberation. Knowing how much she'd been through, the loss of her son and the fact she was on medication for her anxiety, I worried about her more than I would admit to anyone. But seeing her future shining in her face and how much she looked forward to her wedding had me wishing both she and my ex the very best.

Bella settled a little when Brin took possession of her carrier, rubbing herself against the mesh in an attempt to escape and, no doubt, create enough sympathy to convince the young woman to let her out.

"I've got her," Brin said to me, turning to go with the girls, their chatter as they followed the porter and our luggage so lovely, I almost missed it.

Blame it on my natural curiosity or cynicism or fate. Whatever you like, pick one, because ultimately it didn't matter why I looked up and noticed the man lurking on the other side of the towering column outside the main doors, an artfully placed Christmas tree flanking said column to provide cover. All I registered in that moment of awareness was the expression on his face.

Someone had made him very unhappy and that someone was one of the girls.

All kinds of terrifying scenarios unwound in my head in the flash of a moment it took for me to realize he was a potential threat. I'd been through enough threats to my own life, let alone Thalia and Callie, that I guess I was (and always would be) on high alert when it came to any chance of attack. And yes, I know I jumped to conclusions because of previous trauma I was working on, thank you very much, but the intensity of malice I saw on that strange man's face had me immediately changing course and heading right for him.

Was he an assassin, someone sent to kill Thalia because of Gaines and his profession? Or a threat to Callie because of Trent's work as an FBI agent who hunted and captured serial killers and other horrible people? My foot just touched the bottom step, the girls already way ahead of me and almost to the doors, before the man realized I was there. His gaze dropped as they disappeared inside, falling to me and the motion of my approach. With shock replacing his visible anger, he spun and hurried away. By the time I made it to the place where he'd hovered to watch the girls, he was long gone.

But not forgotten. Oh, no. Momma Bear was on the case now and he'd better watch *out*.

At least his rapid retreat had me somewhat mollified. It wasn't lost on me as I carried on inside in pursuit of the girls that I'd just thrown myself in the path of someone who could have killed me and made sure the body was never found without a second thought. The fact he'd run from me like a coward convinced me whatever he was up to, whoever he was, the chances he was a professional of the murderous variety was now doubtful. Still, I made a note to myself if I spotted him again to take a photo and report him to security, just in case.

The girls already had us checked in by the time I joined them. I'd originally planned a room of my own, but they'd convinced me to use their suite which gave me my own bedroom and bathroom anyway, so I'd agreed, if initially reluctantly because if Boone did accept my invitation, I didn't want to have to explain myself. Ahem. However, now that it seemed some measure of vigilance was necessary, I was glad for the arrangements.

And the fact Cherise King was just down the hall.

But it wasn't my tall, Amazonian ex-FBI sheriff friend who came rushing toward me and hugged me in great enthusiasm. Another shock, Melanie Anderson let me go with a beaming smile and so much joy on her face everything in me softened. I'd only ever wanted Trent's happiness, I swear. That was the whole reason I divorced him, to free him to find someone he deserved and who deserved him. I'd had brief moments of doubt about Melanie, but all of that dissolved one last time as she hugged me again.

"I'm so glad you said yes," she whispered in my ear, letting me go and blinking some tears, still smiling. "I really wanted you to come, Seph. It means so much to me."

"This was *your* idea?" I almost shook my head but held off because she turned and took Callie's hand, pulling my daughter in, Brin and Thalia joining us.

"One big happy family," Melanie said with a tremulous laugh. "This is going to be the best Christmas *ever*."

Everyone hugged while something clicked in my head and when I was included in the embrace, I joined with enthusiasm. It was clear to me that Melanie never had anything of the sort and if I could give her some semblance of that, I was happy to do so.

"Can the maid of honor join in?" I pulled back as another woman spoke, noting the faintly biting tone of her voice, though she was smiling when she said it. I took in the medium height, medium build brunette with her chunky blonde highlights and tight jeans, plethora of silver jewelry and gauzy button-up open to show all of her cleavage and am ashamed to admit I judged her.

Melanie turned to her and dragged her into our circle, however, the heavy scent of the woman's perfume sickly sweet and making my nose itch. The embrace didn't last, a faint awkwardness seeming to settle around all of us, though Melanie carried on regardless, holding the newcomer's hand.

"Carla Helland," she said, "this is Persephone Pringle."

"The ex," Carla said, again with that biting tone behind her smile. Classy. Not.

I shook her hand, her rings pinching my skin as she squeezed. "Nice to meet you," I said, stepping back to allow Melanie to introduce Callie and Thalia, wanting to observe. Carla's attitude wasn't redeeming her in the least, arrogance mixed with visible jealousy as she complimented Thalia's jacket but looked at it with an acquisitiveness that had my protectiveness fired up all over again. "Carla and I have been best friends since childhood." Melanie pulled the other woman into her with one arm around her shoulders.

"We should let them get settled," Carla said. "And start getting you ready for the rehearsal dinner tonight. You have a massage in ten minutes." It sounded great but why then did it also seem like Carla was chastising her? Not my problem and not my friend. Her flat stare when she caught my eye that then forced itself into pleasantness churned my stomach.

"Right." Melanie nodded to her, hugging each of us again. "Brin, honey, are you coming?"

13

They trooped off while the porter led us through the lobby to the elevators. Our suite, it turned out, was in a separate block of the hotel at the far back, so it took a bit to navigate there. But when I walked through the door into our room and looked out over the balcony to the garden below, it was worth it.

Thalia had already tipped the porter and he was on his way out as Callie threw herself down on the white leather sofa, a blotch of red in the pristine puffiness. "This is perfect." I nodded, taking in the giant marble fireplace, the fur rugs thrown over the matching marble floors, the small dining area, crystal chandelier lighting the white and silver room. Someone had decorated for Christmas with tasteful splashes of red and silver, the tall, narrow tree next to the fireplace glittering and glowing. Further exploration of the doorways on either end of the room revealed a large master with ensuite and a king-sized bed with the second the same setup but a queen that I was happy to claim.

I had just loosed Belladonna to explore when someone knocked on the main door. I greeted Trent as I opened it, my ex quickly bending to capture my cat as she tried to scoot out between my legs. He instantly sneezed while I took her from him, ushering him inside, locking her in my bedroom before returning to him with a tissue.

"I'm fine," he said, dabbing at his running eyes, recovering somewhat as he went on. His allergies had always prevented me from having a pet, another benefit to our divorce, as far as I was concerned. He didn't visit much despite our amicability, and I was just fine with that arrangement. "Thanks for coming, Seph. It means a lot to Melanie."

I took in my middle-height, unassuming-looking ex-husband, his round cheeks and hazel eyes the mirror of our daughter and felt a wave of affection flow through me. Not love, not like that. But we'd shared a lot together, had a child, experienced many ups and downs in our years as a couple. Trent had never done anything to hurt me outside our incompatibility. Quite the opposite, in fact, our lack of connection merely personality based and obvious in hindsight. So, there were no grudges and though I knew we had so little in common we were never destined to be friends, I could be genuinely happy for him and the simple, quiet joy I saw in his face.

I hugged him, felt his tension dissolve and him embrace me back for a moment before I let him go. "Congratulations," I said. "You deserve to be loved the way she loves you."

Trent cleared his throat after a moment, looking down then up again. "Thank you," he said. For what, he didn't specify, but I had to believe, as he held my hand and stared into my eyes for a long moment that carried far more meaning than those two simple words, that he was finally grateful I'd done what he begged me not to.

How awesome was that?

CHAPTER THREE

We both laughed after a bit, Trent dropping my hand. "She's going to be a bit much the next two days," he said. My ex was notoriously underemotional and I could only imagine how much Melanie's enthusiasm was making him uncomfortable, though he seemed softly pleased by the fact. "She's never really had a family before. She keeps talking about all of us coming together regularly." Oh, dear. He waved off my inhale as I planned to protest. "Don't worry," he said, "I'm not into that either." We grinned at one another. "And, if I can give her this little thing, make her happy, I will."

He was such a good person. And while I'd been very irritated with him over the last few months

16

because of his intense focus on Melanie and Brin to what I thought was the detriment of his relationship with our daughter, I let all that go as the girls rushed out of their bedroom to hug Trent and chatter at him while I retreated.

Bella glared at me from the bed, hunched in a fluffy hump, tail wrapped around her paws as she crouched and muttered.

"You can just behave yourself, young lady," I shot back. "You can do two days, bratski. Don't make me chase you."

She grumbled a bit more before lying down and continuing to glare.

I took the time we had before the 6PM rehearsal dinner to enjoy a long, delicious soak in the giant tub in my bathroom before curling up by the fire with a book as the girls ran out to explore the hotel. Bella relented, climbing into my lap and curling up to sleep though when Callie and Thalia returned at 5PM, my cat disappeared under the bed and wouldn't come out.

Well, she had litter and food and water, the silly thing. And I left her a little pile of her favorite treats, too. If she wanted to sulk, she could go ahead and do so. I had a party to attend and would snuggle her later and make up for her confinement.

I was a bit concerned the red velvet dress I'd chosen might be too much but seeing Callie in her gold lamé pantsuit and Thalia in a deep blue satin sheath, both sporting updos, made me feel better, if a bit old.

We were almost to the elevator when a door

opened and a tall, stunning black woman emerged, black velvet suit matched with a silk shell of the same color making her look like a supermodel. Cherise King squealed like a girl when she saw me, hugging me, her husband, Martin, equally as statuesque and stunning joined us, not quite in a tux but gorgeous in his dark suit and deep red button up.

Their daughter, Layla bounced out into the hall, slightly younger than Callie and Thalia but no less a good friend, though it had aways been obvious to me she held both young women as role models. It was clear from the way she oohed and ahhed over both of them and their outfits that hadn't changed, though Layla herself looked amazing in her black and silver dress with her shining corkscrew curls left natural around her lovely face.

"You made it." Cherise winked at me, full lips dark red and shining, a touch of gold liner around her eyes making her look exotic.

I shrugged as the elevator dinged and we all entered. "Free dinner," I said.

Cherise chuckled. "Is he coming?" She didn't have to caveat the "he" for me, did she? I caught myself blushing and snapped her with the edge of my clutch purse with a wicked grin fighting for control of my face.

"Haven't heard yet." I shot her a "hush, woman" look that made her laugh again and worried she might carry on with questions I couldn't answer in this company. Not that I was hiding my growing relationship with Boone from Callie or anything, but I wasn't being overt about it and preferred to keep it that way.

Cherise knew better, though her own wickedness wasn't going anywhere. "Keep me posted." Since she knew Boone personally, I inwardly groaned at her insider knowledge while sighing like a teenager over the gorgeous man I really hoped I hadn't chased off with my offer.

Grow up, Persephone Pringle.

I had no idea where we were going, but apparently, I was the only one, so I was content to follow the others, ending up in a small but lovely private dining room. This one had been heavily decorated for Christmas, but it had also been augmented with what was likely a variety of Valentine's Day items the hotel had on hand because it felt like Cupid had thrown up all over Santa's spilled gift bag and the pair had called it a day.

Melanie and Trent greeted us at the door, our places all preselected, and I found myself sitting in a chair covered in a fluffy red and white faux-wool cover between Cherise and Callie. Directly across from me sat a handsome middle-aged man who looked vaguely familiar. He held out his hand, smiling at me, dark hair clipped into regulation FBI condition with enough silver in it to catch the light, pale brown skin and deep brown eyes making him of Latino origin.

"SSA Angelo Flores," he said as he released my hand. "We met once a few years ago at a company Christmas party. I'm an old friend of Trent's."

"Of course, Agent Flores," I said, not really remembering. "Lovely to see you again."

"You too, Ms. Pringle," he said. "Call me Angelo."

"Seph." I nodded toward Trent as he gently pushed in Melanie's chair for her. She'd chosen a bright red dress that was a bit too orange to suit her skin tone but from the look of my ex and his doting attention he thought she was the most beautiful woman on the planet. I caught a flicker of what looked like jealousy on Carla's face as the maid of honor sat, her hair in a rather elaborate updo that showcased her streaks of blonde, the epically tight black bandage dress she wore straining as she settled.

"I've joined Trent's unit," Angelo said, drawing my attention back. "He heard I was leaving my current position and invited me to be on his team. It's been an amazing six months. We really reconnected."

Oh, he was explaining why he was invited to the wedding, obviously. "What division were you in before?"

"No work talk, please." Trent interrupted me. Normally I would have been irritated by it. He had this way of making me feel chastised and silenced that drove me nuts on a normal day. Tonight, however, I let it go immediately, proud of myself for how far I'd come, and sat back to give him the floor.

Trent held up a glass, all of ours previously filled with what had to be champagne, and we lifted the delicate crystal in salute as he turned to Melanie.

"Mel," he said, "my friends and family," he nodded to all of us, "thank you so much for coming to celebrate our wedding." Trent wasn't much of a speech maker, so this was a huge thing for him and even if his actual words weren't poetic, the energy behind them certainly was. "I'm the luckiest man alive." He turned back to his bride-to-be who was smiling up at him with great tenderness and a trembling lower lip. "I love you so much. Meeting you was the best thing that ever happened to me, and I can't wait to spend the rest of our lives together." She clasped her hands over her heart, gaze never leaving his, while I caught Carla's eye roll. And while it was gushy and mushy, sure, they were getting married. Weren't maids of honor supposed to be happy for the bride?

"To Melanie," Trent said, drinking. I sipped my champagne while Melanie stood.

"My love," she said, kissing Trent before turning to all of us, cheeks flushed, eyes full of tears. "It means so much to both of us that you are here to witness our wedding. You say you're the luckiest man alive," she turned to Trent again, "but you've made me the happiest I've ever been, and I can't imagine my life without you." They kissed again while we all cheered before Melanie raised her glass. "To Trent."

I set down my drink as Trent again helped his bride-to-be sit, official toasts over, apparently, as the wait staff began bringing in salads. To my surprise, the food was excellent, not normal wedding rehearsal fare, not a scrap of rubber chicken or overdone veggies in sight. In fact, I not only ate every bite of the delicious courses offered, I imbibed of enough gin and laughter and contentment that I had to excuse myself partway through the main and dessert delivery to find the ladies' room.

While the dining room was private, it wasn't far from the main lobby, so I found myself passing along the far end of the foyer following signs to the washrooms. Wouldn't you know, the moment I pushed through, I realized I'd have a bit of a wait, the lineup at least ten women long and making me grumbly about the fact the men's was probably empty.

I was about to turn and give it a go—I'd had enough gin to do so, trust me—when a hand grasped for my arm as someone stumbled into me.

"Oh, I beg your pardon," the elderly woman said, breathing a little heavily. "Is there a line?"

I supported her instantly. "I was just going to use the men's," I said.

She smiled up at me with a tight grin. "Oh, yes," she said. "Let's."

With a willing partner in crime at my side, I laughed with my new companion and did just that.

CHAPTER FOUR

"I love your hair," my elderly friend said while we exited into the hallway again and I turned toward the men's room. She thudded her silver cane's heavy rubber end on the carpeting, her clear blue eyes taking me in. "And your tattoos. What a lovely young woman you are."

"A few years past young," I winked at her.

"My dear," she said, "when you get to my age, everyone is young."

I took in the startled expression on the man's face who was striding out as we walked in, his confusion brushed off by my elderly companion as she waved her cane at him.

"Out with you," she said, commanding tone sending him scurrying. "There we are." She turned

23

back and slid her cane through the handle of the door so it couldn't be pulled outward, grinning up at me with another saucy wink. "If you'd be so kind."

I supported her to the far stall and took the one next, out again quickly and helping her to the sink, washing my hands and staying with her as she wobbled somewhat.

"Old is fine," she said, "as long as you're healthy."

"You seem like you're doing great to me," I said. "And I love your dress." It was adorable on her, her petite body artfully draped in black satin and lace, gorgeous flashes of diamonds that had to be real adorning a choker around her neck and a thick bracelet at her wrist. One single solitaire sat on her thin ring finger.

"One does love to make an impression," she said, before offering me a tiny vial of something from her clutch. I accepted a dollop of cream and rubbed it into my hands, immediately in love with the soft scent and marveling at how my skin felt. "Stella Gannister, how rude of me."

"Persephone Pringle," I answered. "I'm just as rude, it seems." I gestured to the door. "Shall we let the men have their room back?"

She winced a little, motioning instead to the small divan in the entryway of the bathroom. "A moment, if you don't mind," she said. "To rest my feet."

I helped her to sit immediately, surprised no one had tried to enter yet, perching next to her. She held my hand as I did, patting it gently before letting me go.

"Are you here for Christmas with your family?" Maybe I could fetch someone for her.

She shook her head, sighing a little. "Unfortunately, no," she said. "I fled that wretched pack of greedy wolves, may they all wail their despair that grandmother has escaped them this year." I caught a laugh despite the sadness of the matter, Stella leaning forward to poke me with narrowed eyes and her grin firmly in place. "Now, don't you pity this old woman. I like my solitude after all this time. Besides, their whining gives me indigestion." Stella sat back, perfectly styled white curls sparkling on the right side with a small diamond hairpiece I was sure was real, too. "And you, Persephone Pringle?"

"My ex-husband is getting married," I said. Laughed when her eyebrows shot up. "I'm happy for him."

"My ex-husband died in the arms of a prostitute," she said, making me snort in surprise and appalled humor as she went on. "Exactly how he wanted to go, so everyone was happy."

Her outrageousness made me hope I'd turn out like her when I was an old lady. "No harm then," I said.

Stella's smile tightened. "Not to me."

We laughed together and I found myself adoring her already.

"I do hope Santa finds you," I said.

"There's little I want for Christmas, dear," she said then, sighing softly, wriggling her feet in her low pumps. "If you ever reach my age, you'll discover few things matter anymore." When she looked up and met my eyes again, hers were intense and focused. She might have been elderly and her body giving her issues, but there wasn't a thing wrong with her mind. "With all said and done, only one thing really has import, Persephone." I expected her to say love or gratitude or something similar. Instead, she snorted. "Good gin and someone to drink it with."

Okay, I laughed again because she was my kind of woman. "I'll remember that."

"Very well then, dear," she said. "Help me up?"

I did, guiding her to her feet before leaving her a moment to free her cane from the door and return it to her. She brandished it like a weapon before her, then thudded the end into the tile. "Are they happy?" There was an almost plaintive note to Stella's question that had me hesitate.

"Who?" I helped her shuffle her way to the exit, her arm in mine.

"Your ex and his bride-to-be." I opened the door and let Stella go ahead of me, staying close.

"Deliriously," I said.

Stella didn't comment until we reached the edge of the lobby. To my surprise, a tall, broad-shouldered man seemed to appear from nowhere, shaved head and heavy brows giving him a rather threatening look, dark suit and frown only increasing my discomfort in his presence as his menacing stare locked on me despite the fact that he kept a bit of distance. Stella noticed me looking and waved off my weird anxiety.

"He's with me," she said before squeezing my

hand. "Thank you, Persephone. I've enjoyed our chat and your assistance. I hope to see you again." She snapped her fingers. "Domino, your arm, please."

He was at her side so fast I barely saw him move, almost liquid in his motions, silent and creepy, stealthy even despite his size. His dark brown eyes fixed me with one last look before he led Stella away and I found myself watching them go.

Well, she was obviously rich, so having a manservant wasn't exactly a stretch, though he had more the air of a bodyguard to me than anything. None of my business, either, despite my piqued curiosity. Then again, from what little I'd learned of Stella, maybe I shouldn't have been surprised to find she needed muscle. The way she talked about her family, she could easily have been someone who required guarding after all.

As I turned with more questions than answers, I quickly forgot all about my brief encounter with the remarkable older woman. Not because she was forgettable, to the contrary. No, it was the sight of the same man from earlier in the day, the very one whose lurking and glaring had fired off my warning radar that had me suddenly stiff and anxious all over again.

CHAPTER FIVE

This time I did take a photo, fumbling out my phone and snapping a quick shot of him where he sat on the very edge of the lobby's guest area, eyes glued on the passage leading to the private room where my family and friends had gathered. Maybe he had good reason to be there, and I was overreacting. That was very possible, but I had enough gin in me that I didn't care at the moment. He was going to tell me what he was up to, or I was going to have security haul him out and dump him on the mountain.

At least, that was my intent. He noted my attention just as Callie, Thalia and Brin emerged, heading my way, the man leaping to his feet and shooting the three girls a look so threatening I sped up, only to then turn and hurry off out of my sight.

I had almost reached the end of the hall and the lobby myself when Callie caught my arm and pulled me back, the three girls' smiles and chatter dying off.

"Mom, what's wrong?" I tsked as I stopped and met Callie's eyes, noting the wariness there, the worry.

And made a decision. "Nothing," I said, waving off her skepticism. "Someone was rude, that's all." I exhaled slowly, putting my phone away. At least I had a picture.

"Mom," Callie shook her head at me, "you know what you're like when you're drinking gin."

I scowled at my daughter, because I was far from drunk, thank you. "Where are you heading?" No way was I letting them out of my sight.

"Bathroom," Callie said, nose wrinkling. "Why?"

"I'll join you." I did, following Thalia and Brin inside, Callie still suspicious.

"Weren't you just here?" My daughter caught my arm, the lineup now gone and her companions choosing stalls, giving us a moment. "Is there something?"

I shook my head, jaw tight. "Let's get back for dessert, okay?"

She finally sighed and did as I said. I followed the three as they returned to the dining room, looking back over my shoulder to check for the watcher, but didn't see him again and chose to let it go. That was, until I returned to my seat. The moment Callie was distracted by Thalia on her other side, I leaned into Cherise and showed her the photo. A few quick whispered sentences and she was filled in on the situation.

"I'll keep an eye out," she assured me.

"I don't want to make a big deal of it," I said. "It's probably nothing."

"I trust your instincts," my friend assured me. Honestly? I felt so much better when she said it because a small, nasty part of me was in the process of suggesting I was overreacting. Callie's gin comment was eating at me despite the fact I knew better. "We'll keep it down low for now but thanks for the warning."

Okay, then.

Dinner wrapped up quickly after dessert, though I didn't finish my chocolate torte, stomach too clenched. Cherise assured me she was going to look into the problem, but she and Martin ended up heading out with the happy couple. Angelo and Carla followed, leaving me to go with the girls who headed directly to the dance floor of the small club. When I didn't spot the lurker, I left them to dance. Not completely, mind you, seating myself at the bar on the edge of the lobby with a full view of the space, ordering a gin I barely touched and keeping a lookout.

My phone vibrated as I sipped, incoming text drawing my attention.

How was dinner? Boone's question was a welcome distraction.

Delicious, I sent back to him. *How's work?* He'd volunteered to cover the holidays since most of his fellow detectives had families.

Boring, he sent. *I'm more on call than on duty*. The

30

fact he hadn't mentioned my offer felt like pinpricks as I debated bringing it up. Instead, he went first. *What time is the wedding tomorrow?*

6PM, I sent. *Then it's all fireplaces and hot tubs and books and gin.*

Sounds perfect, he sent.

I waited for more, stomach clenched for a different reason. I wasn't prepared, then, for the appearance of Melanie and Carla who entered the other end of the bar, not seeing me as the bride-to-be tried to order a drink, only to have her maid of honor interrupt her. It appeared to me that they weren't on good terms currently, Melanie pulling her arm away from Carla while her so-called best friend hissed something in her face. Melanie burst into tears and fled the bar, Carla going after her, but not before she looked up and saw me watching.

The flat and unfriendly stare she shot me only lasted a moment before she went after Melanie. I briefly considered getting involved because Carla was clearly a piece of work, but it wasn't my problem and poking my nose in?

I had very little doubt my interference would backfire. Let's face it, one big happy family crossed the line at her future husband's ex interfering in her personal life.

With that decision made, I turned back to my phone, only to catch sight of a familiar pair in the lobby, chatting with someone unexpected. Stella Gannister, her hulking bodyguard standing over her, was in deep conversation with none other than my lurker. She tapped him rather firmly on the leg with the end of her cane, his scowl and headshake sullen but he finally turned and headed toward the main doors, exiting the lobby as the elderly woman spun and walked away.

Wait, why was it she looked so much nimbler than the rather feeble if dignified woman who needed my help?

Now pondering the possibilities, I checked in on the girls, saw them still enjoying their dancing, and chose to head to bed. Whoever the lurker was, Stella had sent him packing. Did that mean he was here with her and whatever his issue was it had nothing to do with us after all? Was I really jumping at shadows?

Gin done and Boone now silent, I chose to return to my room and get some sleep and stop being a silly busybody. This was supposed to be a vacation for me, too, and my nosiness was not going to ruin this trip for me or anyone else.

Trent would never forgive me.

I was just about to open the door to my suite when it whipped wide, a rather panicked young man on the other side. His dark suit and nametag identified him as staff, the small young woman in the maid's outfit behind him who cowered, weeping, near the door boded very badly for what he was about to say.

"I'm so sorry for the intrusion, Ms. Pringle," he said. "Yuri Ellsworth, night manager."

I nodded to him, focusing on the crying maid. "What's happened?"

"She's gone," the girl said, hands shaking.

"Who?" A horrible moment of clarity hit me before she even answered because I knew exactly who, didn't I?

"Your cat," the girl wailed. "She ran away!"

CHAPTER SIX

I think the entire staff of the hotel was conscripted to assist in searching at one point or another that night, the poor maid who Bella bamboozled hunting the most faithfully of all, though no one even spotted the escaped cat, not even Thalia and Callie who returned shortly after my discovery. With Cherise, Martin, Layla and Brin assisting, we combed through the entire hotel, often meeting one another with head shakes and hopeful expressions.

I finally sent everyone back to their rooms and carried on alone, the maid's explanation ringing in my head. "I came to prepare your room for the night," the young woman had blubbered to me. "I saw her run out from under the bed and out the door before I could stop her. I'm so sorry!" Exactly what I'd feared would happen.

I'd be furious with Belladonna if I wasn't so worried.

When I found myself stumbling over my own feet, I finally admitted defeat and headed back to the suite, falling into bed without washing my face or taking off my dress, waking in the early morning with a horrible feeling that evolved into the reminder that my cat had abandoned me. I took a few minutes to have a good cry and feel sorry for myself before hauling myself to the bathroom and cleaning myself up.

She'd made her choice and unless she wanted to be found, she was on her own.

Yes, I was very aware of how that sounded, and of course, I would continue looking. But Bella and I clearly had a conflict when it came to her need for freedom. I couldn't blame her since she'd been practically feral for the first year of her life when her original owner was killed, so being trapped inside wasn't her favorite. Still, she'd seemed so content and loved to help me with clients. Her penchant for escaping was hardly new, just more aggressive and insistent. Whatever her reasons for wanting liberation, I now had that anxiety to carry around with me for the duration of my stay or until she turned up.

Thanks for that, cat.

I joined the girls in the living room, the small pile of gifts they'd brought to exchange a surprise. I'd forgotten it was Christmas in all the mess and hurriedly retrieved the ones I'd packed to add to the stack.

It didn't take long, and it was a subdued process, both Callie and Thalia worried about Bella. I thanked them both for the gorgeous leather gloves that matched my new blue jacket and did my best to smile when they opened identical chokers that I'd bought them they'd admired openly at a local fair. We'd agreed to keep it small, partly because Thalia was rich enough to buy this hotel and partly due to the fact none of us needed anything but one another.

But when Thalia accidentally opened the small box containing the new collar I'd purchased for Bella, she broke into tears and our little charade was all over.

My bout of crying? Happened again, but this time with companionship.

Our breakfast arrived, and food helped, as did coffee, though I was still tired and feeling wonky from being up prowling most of the night.

"We'll find her, Mom," Callie said, squeezing my hand.

"You two are supposed to go skiing," I protested.

"I just *can't*," Thalia shook her head at me, huge eyes wide. "Not knowing Bella is out there on her own."

Having the time of her life, no doubt. The brat.

I felt equally terrible the girls cancelled their plans as I was appreciative of the two of them, Brin and Layla both pitching in to keep searching. I drew my line in the sand at Cherise and Martin ruining their day, however, since they so rarely had time together.

"Go ski," I told my friends. "Have fun for me, okay?"

They went, though Cherise reluctantly, while I set my determination to tracking down that darned cat and locking her up for the rest of her lives (however many she had left). We split up, Callie and Thalia heading out with Brin and Layla teaming up while I set out on my own. I just made it to the lobby with the intent of asking the manager for permission to look in the staff quarters when I ran into none other than Stella Gannister.

"Dear Persephone," she said with raised brows, now dressed in a tidy green suit, "whatever is the matter?"

I filled her in on the missing furchild, Domino listening in while Stella murmured consolations.

"Why, the silly creature," she said. "We'll keep our eyes peeled, won't we, Domino?" He nodded immediately, though didn't speak while Stella patted my hand. "I do hope she's all right, Persephone. What a terrible business. And on Christmas Day, no less."

"She better be," I said. "Thank you, Stella." I paused, question on my mind, but the old woman had carried on and there wasn't a subtle way of asking her who the lurker was she'd spoken to the night before or what his problem was, so I let it go.

I didn't search the whole day, the general manager's kindness and caring unhelpful ultimately, taking a few breaks for lunch and for a short nap so I didn't drop, but other than that, I spent most of

Christmas wandering the hotel calling for Bella. I'm sure I looked like a lunatic, though most people who asked were understanding and agreed to let me know if they spotted her, so at least I succeeded in rousing the entire hotel to be on the lookout.

Not that it mattered. Wherever Belladonna had gotten herself off to, it was apparent by the time 5PM rolled around she wasn't going to be found unless she wanted to be. The horrifying thought someone took her, and she was already long gone only made my heart ache, as did the idea she had somehow gotten outside and was lost out there in the endless forests of the White Mountains drove me to keep searching until the last possible moment.

That meant I only had time for a hasty shower and was the last to arrive at the same small room where we'd dined the night before, now decorated with a white gauze arch, red carpet running to the makeshift altar at the far end. I slipped into the back behind Melanie who was already going inside, wincing as I did my best to avoid her entrance and managing to tuck myself in just before the doors closed behind her.

Not that anyone was looking at me, Melanie's appearance in her lovely white sleeveless lace dress and trailing veil more than enough to distract from my tardiness. Soft strains of an orchestral piece I didn't recognize ushered her down the aisle, radiant and smiling, to join Trent in his tuxedo. Cherise had opted for a matching tux, Carla's gown making me stare as I realized the maid-of-honor also wore white, a tight sheath of layered sequins that made her sparkle like a cake topper. Well, the cheek. Not that it mattered, and she had to know it from her sour expression, because Melanie was the belle of this particular ball, even if only to the man she loved.

That, obviously, was the point, right?

My phone buzzed, fortunately on vibrate, and I quickly checked it to find a message from Boone.

Have fun at the wedding. Was that sarcasm? Hard to know from a line of text.

I'm here now, I sent back. *But I might have a case for you.*

Groan, he texted. *What happened?*

A missing furson. I filled him in on Bella's escape.

I'm so sorry, Seph, he sent. *I hope she shows up.* A short pause followed. *I hope you like your present.*

Wait, my what? We hadn't talked about getting one another presents for Christmas. I hadn't gotten him anything. Before I could inquire, I heard the officiant speak up and, feeling guilty, jammed my phone back in my clutch and paid attention to the reason I was here in the first place.

"If anyone should know of a reason these two should not wed," he said, "speak now—"

Okay, so you always kind of expect an interruption when the ceremony gets to this part, right? Or was that just me? It just seemed like such an open-ended invitation to disaster. Why was it even tradition? Regardless, I have to say I was still shocked when the door to the room slammed open and a man strode inside.

Not just any man, either. The lurker. With a fistful of paperwork that he held up as he spoke.

"I have reason," he said.

Melanie gasped, going so pale I worried she might pass out, Brin spinning with a furious expression.

"You!" Melanie's daughter lunged for him, only Martin King's proximity keeping her from launching herself into a battle, Cherise's tall husband acting immediately to hold Brin back. "What are you doing?"

"You can't marry her," the man said as Melanie shook her head, shaking hand over her open mouth while Trent gaped at him. "She's still married to me."

Oh.

Dear.

CHAPTER SEVEN

"Gerald." Melanie gasped his name, staggering a little, Trent holding her up while she seemed to wobble before catching herself. When she spoke again, she choked before she could go on. "Please, don't do this."

"It's all here in black and white." He tossed the papers to the floor at Trent's feet, grinning with vicious intent. He topped my ex by a few inches, but not much and from his softer appearance didn't spend his weekends training for triathlons. Nor did I suspect he was involved in the kind of law enforcement—if any—that demanded the best of Trent Garret, so I didn't think much of Melanie's ex—oh, dear, *current*—husband if push came to a punch in the face.

41

Which, from the expression that crossed Trent's in that moment, was about to happen. While my mind whirled over the fact that the mild-mannered and unemotional man I'd been wed to for so long could even entertain that kind of reaction let alone show it, I did my best to circle around to the couple, flanking Gerald on one side while Cherise did so on the other, Martin corralling the young women in the group and keeping them out of harm's way. Angelo seemed stunned and unable to respond, though was that a smirk on Carla's face?

If it was? More than one fist would be flying.

"You signed the papers, you swore you did." Melanie shook so badly one of her pinned curls came loose, bouncing over her shoulder and catching on the lace of her neckline. Her full skirt rustled as she sobbed softly before speaking again. "I *saw you* sign."

"But I never filed." He gestured at the pages like they were his greatest accomplishment. Angelo finally snapped out of it, bending to retrieve them and handing them over to Martin King when the lawyer gestured. It only took one look for him to glance up again with a grim expression and a headshake.

"They're not stamped," he said. "We'll have to confirm with county records to be sure."

Well, crap.

"You'll pay for this." Brin's snarl of rage was met with a barking laugh as her father pointed his index finger at her and fake-shot her with a wink.

"No, your mother will." He returned his attention to Melanie whose eyes bulged somewhat, still pale but for two very red marks on her cheeks, blotches climbing down her neck into her décolletage. I didn't cry pretty, but she was a mess. "I told you, Mel. I promised you I'd get the money someday. Now, either you hand over my share or I'll make sure you never get to marry this fine upstanding member of the FBI." His laugh was so harsh and hurtful I didn't blame Trent when he took his turn lunging at the party crasher.

Cherise moved faster and, towering over her smaller friend and former fellow agent, held Trent back. Meanwhile, my mind churned around Gerald's demands in confusion.

"What is he talking about, Mom?" It was Brin who asked the question that had to be on everyone else's mind too. Melanie didn't answer, so Gerald did.

"Your dear mother's been holding out on me, kid," he said, "and you, too." He prodded his daughter with one finger. Or, tried to. The moment he reached for Brin, Martin stiffened, glaring. And while the big family lawyer wasn't a cop or an agent—and was honestly one of the sweetest and gentlest men I knew—there was no doubt in my mind he'd be using that college linebacker physique of his to good use if Gerald tried it again.

Not that Melanie's (ex)husband seemed to care, drawling on as he turned and addressed all of us in a slow spin as he spoke, scruffy face twisting, beady eyes intent, attempt at a respectable suit straining over the round of the potbelly that pushed against the middle button. "She has a trust fund, people. A big one. She's been hiding it for years, refuses to share it. And when I found out about it, she lied. But I know the truth." He finished his spin, pointing at her. "I talked to the source. So, what do you say, Mel? Where's my cut?"

None of this made any sense, really. Melanie had never shown any outward sign of having money. In fact, she worked very hard at her catering business to make ends meet, from what I knew. Then again, we weren't exactly besties, but from what Callie told me, that was the case. If she had access to the kind of money that attracted the attention of filth like him, surely she wouldn't be fighting tooth and nail to save her business on the regular?

Melanie didn't respond, just shaking her head, tucking her face into Trent's shoulder. He seemed to hold her by default, all attention on the man in front of him while Gerald reached into his jacket pocket. Trent immediately reacted, Melanie pushed behind him, Angelo and Cherise both trigger shy and lunging. But Gerald simply extracted a slim set of further paperwork he handed to Trent.

"If she won't share willingly," he said, "she'll do it under a judge's order. See you in court." Gerald laughed as he left, helping himself to a glass of champagne already poured and waiting by the door, a handful of appetizers swiped from the tray beside it as he strolled out like he was king of the world.

And hadn't just ruined everything. No, wait, correction. Was delighted he had.

No one said anything for a long, horrible moment until the officiant sighed deeply, the older man removing his glasses to polish them on his jacket.

"I'm sorry," he said while Melanie wavered further, Trent now holding her up but no longer embracing her, both hands stiff on her upper arms, "but until this is sorted out, I simply can't complete the ceremony."

He exited to the sound of Melanie wailing while Trent's eyes lifted to mine, despair so deep and agonizing I had to look away.

My very Merry Christmas thought upon arrival had surely cursed us all. First Bella now this.

So much for a happy ending.

CHAPTER EIGHT

The moment Gerald was gone, the room broke into loud chatter, Cherise still holding Trent back while Carla comforted Melanie. I approached the poor woman with obvious intent, my particular skillset likely the best option for her at the moment, only to have her maid of honor glare at me with flat dislike.

"Stay out of this," Carla snapped at me. "You're only here as a courtesy." She then guided Melanie toward the exit while I gaped like she'd slapped me.

It kind of felt like she had.

"He swore he'd ruin your life," Brin's voice rose above everyone else's, though she was talking to her retreating mother. Melanie never even lifted her head as Carla hurried her out, Brin turning to Trent. "He's

46

a horrible person and nothing brought him more pleasure than hurting her." Brin tossed her hands, jerking away from Martin who tried to reach for her. "I hate him, and I wish he was dead!" She ran sobbing from the room as well, leaving the rest of us to try to collect ourselves while a seed of warning woke inside me.

Please, not another dead body. It was Christmas.

I took one look at Trent's broken expression and almost went to him, but Cherise had it covered, pulling him aside and sitting him down, speaking low and soft to him while Angelo strode from the room. I hugged both of my girls, Thalia trembling and Callie enraged, before sending them to comfort Trent while I turned and headed after Brin.

She was not going to commit murder and ruin my holiday. Her father had already done enough, thank you.

As I passed the edge of the lobby, I noted Gerald hadn't left the building this time, but was in heated conversation with Angelo. Good, I hoped Trent's friend and partner was giving the loser a piece of his mind. The men parted ways, Angelo heading for the elevators while Gerald seemed intent on the bar, and I almost followed the lowlife. Instead, knowing there was nothing I could do, I carried on with my plan to keep his own daughter from ending his worthless days. She may not have killed anyone before, but I'd seen her rage on a previous occasion and was confident under the right circumstances Brin Anderson would be a danger to herself and others.

These seemed to be those circumstances.

Two elevators arrived at the same moment, and I was about to get on the far right one when Carla hurried off to the far left. She didn't notice me, beelining her way toward the lobby and, curious (and yes, looking for dirt, because I was positive that she was up to no good), I followed. Imagine my surprise when she entered the bar and quickly walked all the way to the back corner booth? It took a bit of wrangling to position myself at the entrance within view of the table in question without being overt or obvious, but my timing was perfect. As I paused behind a Christmas tree partially blocking the doorway, I tilted my head just enough to see who Carla had been so intent on meeting.

Not just meeting, either. If their passionate embrace was any indication, not only had this whole thing been planned but whatever was going on between Carla and Gerald wasn't new. The fact my suspicions the maid of honor in this little drama had been up to no good were confirmed wasn't helping matters, though. Yes, I needed to tell Melanie, clearly, but the timing? Terrible. Knowing her so-called best friend was snogging her not-quite ex after he ruined the wedding was vital information if gossip was the goal. But would it help matters now? I had to consider the emotional impact on Melanie.

And decided there would be time to tell her after the mess was cleaned up and Gerald given the heave-ho, if only to rid Melanie's life of deceit.

That didn't mean I shouldn't tell Trent, however, though the same thought bubbled up. Did he really need this right now? It wasn't exactly a criminal investigation and so what if Carla was part of the plot to ruin the wedding? If she got in my way, on the other hand… I whipped out my phone and took a few pics, feeling very much the voyeur but knowing I'd regret it if I didn't. No way was it going to come down to Carla's word against mine when the time was right.

My phone vibrated as I snapped the last shot, text landing from Melanie. *Can you come? I need someone to talk to.*

I immediately responded to the affirmative and headed back to the elevators, the short walk to the honeymoon suite from my own reminding me of my hunt for Belladonna. Terrible things came in threes, didn't they? No, I wouldn't think like that. Sure, that's why goosebumps traveled over my whole body at the mere idea.

Melanie wasn't alone by the time I arrived, passing Martin and Layla in the hall as they retreated with a sad nod from him and a shoulder shrug from his daughter. I entered the open doorway to find Thalia holding Melanie's hand on one side, Callie on the other while Brin paced—thankfully present and accounted for and not on a homicidal mission— while Trent stood off to one side with Cherise who hovered like she didn't know what to do.

In fact, when my dear friend's dark eyes met mine, there was desperate questioning there. Because I was the one who knew what to do, right? Well, I guess, if only on an emotional level.

Callie and Thalia cleared out when I sat next to Melanie, the poor woman sagging against me, fresh

49

tears falling as she dabbed at the disaster of her makeup with a wad of damp, mascara darkened tissues. "I'm a fool," she croaked.

"It's not your fault," I said. "The papers were signed, Melanie."

"Why did you trust him to file them?" I wasn't expecting Trent to blurt that question, nor the betrayal on his face when she wrung her hands and tried to speak for so long that he let out a grunt of pain and turned away.

Melanie finally found words. "He didn't give me a choice," she told me barely above a whisper, though it was so quiet in the room I knew her voice carried. "He took the papers, promised me he'd file. They were already signed so I believed him."

"You said you checked with the county," Trent said, voice low and vibrating with fury. Blame, too.

"I didn't hear back in time," she wailed. "I tried, Trent, but we decided so quickly and the clerk's office was busy. I was sure it was all right." She choked on more tears before clearing her thick throat. "I'm so sorry. I've ruined everything."

"You have not," I said with enough volume Trent had to know it was meant for him, too. "You did your best. The fact your ex-husband—and I don't care what you say," I shut my own ex down as he turned and tried to protest, "those papers are signed, Trent, so she's not married to him anymore." Trent relented, shoulders sagging as he tossed his hands. A Christmas miracle, at least he was going to let me finish, which I did. "The fact your ex-husband," I repeated for emphasis, "is a total

50

jerkface who purposely did this to hurt you both means nothing about you or your relationship. Or how you feel about one another. Does it?" I looked up as Melanie shook her head, Trent slowly shaking his. "I know it sucks," I said, "but you can either let him win and tear you apart over a ceremony that means nothing because love is more important," so there, "or you can do everything in your power to ruin his plans by choosing to move on with an epic story to tell."

Neither of them said anything, though Melanie looked slightly less upset, so hopefully the truth was getting through.

"I have a friend in Judge Dingwell's office," Cherise said. "Owes me a big favor. I know she can get him to process the divorce papers retroactively to the signed date."

"After the holidays," Trent said. Dear lord, that man and his negativity was going to be the death of him.

Eep, I didn't say that, I swear. But honestly, I'd thought Melanie had helped him shed his pessimism. Apparently not.

"And the lawsuit?" Brin spun on her mother, arms crossed over her chest, belligerence in her jutting jaw, her tight frown, the tapping toes of one foot. "What was Dad talking about, Mom? What money?"

Trent wavered as Melanie hesitated and then sighed deeply, head hanging, no longer leaning into me but rigid and cold.

"It's true," she whispered. Whipped her head up

when Trent swore. We all did, Callie gasping because she may have heard her father say a bad word once in her entire life. In fact, he always gave me a hard time for casual swearing, considered it beneath him. Clearly, that wasn't the case now. "Trent, it doesn't matter."

"It does," he snarled at her, heading for the door. "Because now I need to know what else you've lied to me about." Instead of waiting to find out, however, he slammed his way out of the room, leaving me to once again comfort Melanie as she fell to my shoulder and wept her heart out.

While I worried deeply now not just about Brin and what she might do because I'd never seen my ex so angry and if anyone knew how to commit murder and hide a body...

I was honestly afraid of what he might do.

CHAPTER NINE

Carla's return reminded me of her subterfuge and when she immediately tried to oust me from my place next to Melanie, I almost fought her on it. Until the victim of this heinous day patted my hand with thanks and turned to her lying bestie while I fumed a little and almost did something I knew I'd regret.

Brin's fury distracted sufficiently as she, too, stormed for the door. "I'm going to kill him with my bare hands." I rose and went after her, but Cherise blocked me from following, to my surprise.

"I know," she said, voice low and soft and holding a warning, "but you have to let them deal with this. Seph, no matter what, we both know how this will shake out if you don't back off."

She was right, so right, I'd been thinking it earlier.

Invited guest, extended family, sure, when times were happy, and celebrations were to be had. But the fastest way to make enemies of my ex and his hopeful bride was to do anything at all.

Argh.

We finally dispersed, Carla remaining behind alone with Melanie. That only made my stomach churn and though I longed to share with Cherise, she was already gone behind her own suite's door to rejoin her family, which left me with the sorrowful duo of Callie and Thalia to trail behind into our own suite.

"I'm starving," I said in a brighter tone than was likely warranted, but both girls nodded. "Let's change and order in, shall we?"

Both were amenable, and we quickly donned fluffy Christmas pajamas, dinner arriving within a half hour. While we weren't able to partake in the wedding feast, we weren't left hanging, the hotel providing us with a four-course holiday meal that filled the bill perfectly.

Our deepest apologies, the note with the first tray said, signed by Yuri Ellsworth, the night manager. *Please enjoy this holiday meal on us.*

I debated the entire dinner, considering telling the girls what I'd seen, finally choosing again to keep it to myself. The last thing I wanted was to come across as a gossip and knowing Callie's sensitivity about her father and her accusations against me in the past of not minding my own business, my decision was kind of made for me. We'd already had a stressful twenty-four hours. A big fight with my daughter wasn't how I wanted to cap off this horrible attempt at happiness.

The girls retired early, leaving me to sip gin in front of the fire, but my immobility didn't last long. With the wedding mess in the back of my mind, Bella leaped to the forefront and with a groan of guilt, I was up and heading out to prowl the halls of the hotel again. Yes, in my jammies, and if anyone judged me for it, they could suck it.

I was just about to open my door when I heard voices in the hall around the corner and peeked before imposing.

"I should have known this would happen," Trent was saying to Melanie, his bags in the hallway outside the bridal suite. He didn't yell, that was so Trent. No, instead he used that disappointed voice of his, that judgy and weighty FBI agent voice that always made me furious in its reasonable accusation.

"Trent, please, I love you." Melanie didn't stand a chance against it, hands reaching for him. She was still in her wedding dress, though in wrinkled shambles, Trent now in jeans and a sweater.

"I'm tired of the lies, Mel," he said, crossing the hall and keying a door, going inside and closing the way firmly behind him.

She sobbed, sagging as Carla appeared behind her. Melanie turned to her not-friend. "I can't stay here." She slipped inside, retrieving her own luggage. "I can't believe this is happening!"

Carla guided her down the hall to her own room and the two disappeared within. I let out a long, sad sigh, shaking my head as I slipped out at last and hurried to the corner and around it before anyone saw me. Looked like my attempt to mend fences hadn't worked after all.

Not my problem and nothing I could do about it. Which had me purposely refocusing on what I could do.

Bella, you bratski. The cat was it.

An hour later I had circled back again, the walk making me feel better after stuffing myself at dinner but without any success when it came to finding the missing furchild. I was just reaching the corner to the suites hallway when Brin came hurrying around it and ran into me. I caught her as she cried out, eyes wide and almost afraid as I grasped her and held her in place a moment. She hadn't yet changed out of her dress from the wedding, but like her mother, her makeup was a disaster. She didn't seem to care, pulling away from me when I offered compassion without speaking.

"Leave it," she snapped. "It doesn't matter anymore." She hoofed off, high heels thudding into the carpet runner when she hurried away. The ding of the elevator signaled her departure and I finally turned back to carry on. Only to run into another person who was barreling down the corridor and took the corner too fast.

This time it was Angelo who caught me one handed, his anxious expression turning to concern as he apologized profusely.

"I'm okay," I said with a breathless little laugh. "You?"

He shrugged, letting me go, free hand diving in

the pocket of his pants, the other covered with his jacket draped over his arm. Angelo's head hung down so his dark hair hung over his brown eyes. "Such a mess," he said. "I feel terrible for Trent."

"Did he talk to you?" Maybe another man might be the ticket?

Angelo shook his head, wiping at his mouth with his free hand. "Sorry again. Have a good night, Seph." He carried on while I worried. If Trent wouldn't talk to Angelo either, maybe he'd listen to Cherise? Or Martin? Or maybe he needed time to process. I'd spent enough years with him to know he didn't take sudden change well and liked order and organization. This must have hit him hard in more than just emotional ways. I had to believe once he had time to work through the whole thing he'd be more practical about it.

Again, not my problem. Where was that dratted feline?

As I turned the corner, I paused one last time, though not from impending impact, at least. No, instead, it was the sight of Carla coming out of the bridal suite, scowling and swearing to herself, that had me stopping in my tracks. She didn't see me, hurriedly returning to her own suite and closing the door, forcing me to mind my own business yet again. Yes, I debated knocking and asking her what she was up to, but Melanie was supposedly with her, and that would just raise more questions than I was willing to answer right now.

I passed to the end of the hallway, into the alcove there, looking out the window and hoping Bella was safe and warm inside, the thought that she'd escaped weighing on me now more than ever. My mind conjured images of her wailing in the woods, terrified and freezing, while I wasted time looking around the hotel over and over again.

I'd just turned back, determined to get my coat and tromp around in the snow looking for tracks when another door opened and froze me in place. Fortunately, the alcove had yet another Christmas tree as a decoration, so I was able to blend in behind it. And wince my way through Trent going into the bridal suite. He was only inside a moment, the door closing behind him, when the sound of more swearing made me hesitate to move. I could have tried to comfort him, almost did despite myself. I crept to the door to listen, heard grunting and more swearing, a thudding sound, then nothing. He almost caught me eavesdropping, the tap of his shoes on the floor the only warning I had to dash back to the alcove. Fortunately, Trent was so worked up he likely wasn't seeing anything and stomped down the hallway to the corner and around the bend. Where was he going?

That didn't matter so much, not when a final door opened, to a suite just down the hall. I watched as Stella Gannister emerged, Domino behind her, and the pair helped themselves to the wide-open door to the bridal suite.

CHAPTER TEN

Correction. Only Domino entered the suite, Stella standing guard outside with her silver cane in hand while her tall bodyguard closed the door behind him. The old woman didn't seem even remotely hesitant, face composed and innocent as she leaned against the wall as though resting, both hands folded neatly on the top of her planted cane. I debated interrupting, calling her on the obvious intrusion, only to see Domino exit a moment before I could, shaking his head at his employer who frowned a little and proceeded back to her own room.

That was a lot of activity for a short time period and only one of the people who'd gone inside had the right to be there. Whatever the others had been up to, it was now obvious to me that Stella Gannister was no stranger to this mess my family found themselves in and whatever the old woman's connection, it had to be to Melanie, right?

Curiosity won, because if Stella had something to do with the disastrous wedding, that was far enough outside broken hearts and led me down a more sinister path of concern. Melanie's supposed inheritance and the involvement of who looked to me to be a wealthy older woman was in no way a coincidence now that I'd seen Stella's manservant poking around.

Honestly, my main reason for finally taking action? Doing so beat wandering the halls and worrying about Bella.

I knocked on Carla's door, the woman answering shortly after I did, though she scowled at me when I asked for the key to the bridal suite.

"I told you to stay out of this." She closed the door in my face, but not before I spotted Melanie passed out on the sofa, her back to me, still in her wedding dress. Fine, I had other means. I knocked on Trent's door this time, but he either refused to answer or had passed out himself. More than likely the former.

I had one last means of entry, and I took it, stomping to the front desk and confronting the night manager. Yuri Ellsworth emerged from somewhere out back and paled at the sight of me, though I did calm enough to thank him for dinner.

"I need a key for the bridal suite," I said once he stammered his next apology.

"I see," he said, hesitation not winning him points. The poor guy, I did feel sorry for him, but I was on a mission to distract myself from my lost cat and protect my family just in case and there was no way someone like him was getting in my way.

"I heard meowing, and no one is awake to open the door," I said. "They are my *family*." I stressed that and saw him waver. "It's not like I'll be interrupting anyone. The couple is in different rooms." And I had to go that far, making him wince, but he quickly proffered a key, didn't he?

Never underestimate the power of emotional discomfort.

I waved off Yuri's offer to assist and hit the elevators, quickly back in front of the bridal suite door with my newly procured key. Once inside, I realized what caused all the swearing I'd heard from my normally proper ex-husband, stopping on the threshold with my mouth hanging open.

Someone had trashed the joint. Like, not just made a mess but *trashed*. The layout was similar to the suite I shared with the girls, though there was only one door to the master bedroom. It stood open, revealing that the disaster of the main living room was repeated elsewhere. The lovely fur area rug in front of the fireplace? Had been ripped apart, red rose petals ground into the fibers, a whole bottle of red wine spilled over the white leather sofa. Someone had taken a knife to the upholstery of the matching chair, and for added measure used it on the heavy velvet drapes, shredding them. A box of chocolates had been dumped and smooshed into the bedspread, more wine poured over the pillows. I could only shake my head at the destruction of the side tables, the stained and torn towels and robes, the smashed lamps and broken champagne flutes littering the bathroom floor.

No wonder Trent was so angry. It had to have been Gerald, naturally, though I certainly wasn't putting anything past Carla. The fact I'd seen her exiting this very suite added to her amorous attachment to Melanie's despicable ex, meant she more than likely had a hand in this giant mess. A mess, no doubt, Trent would be financially responsible for.

Yeah, he'd love that. I was surprised Captain Frugal hadn't blown an artery.

I did a half-hearted search for Bella just to cover bases, exiting into the main room and feeling a cold breeze draw me to the sliding glass doors. Someone had decorated the hot tub on the deck, and the lights still glowed around it, an empty bucket meant for a bottle next to the steps. I shivered as a gust of wind hit me, ruffling something on the edge of the tub, catching my attention. Frowning in the low light and faint glow of the small bulbs, I squinted as I approached, head tilting as I tried to figure out what it was that stuck out of the water like that.

And froze, catching my breath before groaning as I finally deciphered the object.

Legs. They were legs, the pants hem fluttering in the breeze, to shiny black shoes draped over the lip of the tub while the rest of whoever it was had sunk under the surface. I felt myself choke up a little, terrified to discover it might be Trent, only to peer down through what was left of the bubbles and floating rose petals into the staring eyes of Melanie's ex.

CHAPTER ELEVEN

I was dialing 9-1-1, hurrying down the corridor toward the elevators, when the doors dinged and the last person I expected to see stepped off. Maine State Police Detective Kellan Boone spotted me the moment his boot hit the carpet, sea-green eyes widening as I rushed toward him, my call forgotten.

"How did you know?" I hugged him tight, releasing him quickly, staring up into those gorgeous eyes while his previously curious expression turned to concern.

"Don't tell me," he said.

I had the good grace to wince. "You're not here for the murder."

Boone sighed, one hand sliding through his dark hair, the silver at his temples catching light, scruff on

64

his jaw sparkling too when he clenched it. That hand fell to his waist, pushing back his short jacket and exposing the shining silver "B" belt buckle he always wore. I'd have taken more time to admire the gorgeousness of his tall, dark delicious nature if I hadn't had a body to show him, but that quick embrace and moment of connection would have to do for the time being.

"Show me," he said, bag swinging at his side as he followed me toward the bridal suite.

Which had me pausing suddenly, turning back to him, one hand on his broad chest to stop him in his tracks. "You came," I whispered then, wonder in my words, unable to stop it.

"Of course, I did," he said, deep voice dropping even further while he cracked a crooked smile. "You didn't have to add murder to make me show up, Seph. I was already on my way."

That was... lovely. And I had to go and make it weird by finding a corpse.

Awesome.

"Merry Christmas," he said, soft kiss landing on my cheek. "You'll get your present later. Right now, I believe you have a gift for me." He grimaced. "You sure know how to show a guy a good time, Pringle."

Not my fault, darn it.

Boone got to work quickly, and by the time I delivered his bag to my room and returned to the bridal suite, he was on the phone to the office, summoning the troops. I had hoped the late hour might mean we could keep things quiet from the others for at least a little bit, but the arrival of a pair of officers, with night manager Yuri Ellsworth at their side, meant the noise level in the hallway took on unusual levels for that late at night and stirred enough curiosity it wasn't long before heads were poking out of doorways.

I grabbed Cherise when she emerged in her robe, yawning and frowning, dragging her to join me as Boone nodded his greeting. Her wicked grin turned to surprise at the sight of two uniforms wading through the mess in the bridal suite, my sheriff friend mimicking Boone's groan when she realized what was going on.

"Tell me you didn't find a body," she said. Then started, dark eyes huge, panic gripping her as she grasped onto me with both big hands. "Trent," she said in a strangled tone.

"Gerald," I reassured her with that name.

"Apparently, someone wasn't happy about Mr. Berman's presence," Boone said in his typical dry tone. Who? Oh, he meant the dead ex. Why did I think his name would have been Anderson? Cherise relaxed somewhat, but her grim expression still held concern.

I knew why, too. Because there was a prime suspect on both of our minds and his name was Trent Garret.

"I'll have to talk to SAIC Garret," Boone said, making it a trio of suspicion.

"I'll go wake him." Cherise turned to do so, only to have my ex walk through the door, expression pinched, stunned. Clearly, Trent had been through enough in the last few hours he was struggling to accept more could be coming, though when his gaze fell on Boone, he tensed instantly. I watched my ex go from flustered to focused, his FBI training obviously kicking in. Trent strode forward and extended his hand, Boone accepting it and shaking it with matched professionalism as my ex spoke.

"What's happened, detective?" They must have encountered one another at some point on their professional paths.

"Kellan Boone, Agent Garret," Boone said. Oh, so no interaction, just a cop recognizing another cop. Gotcha. And phew. Yes, a petty thing to be relieved about but was it wrong I didn't want any history between the man I was married to and the man I was dating?

"Detective Boone," Trent said, looking around with his own grim unhappiness matching Cherise's. "Division?"

"Homicide," Boone said.

Okay, that shook Trent at last. He gaped a moment before turning to me. "Who died?"

I didn't get to answer, not when a short, stocky man in round glasses with a receding hairline and sparkling smile entered the room, waving to me and Boone both.

"Dr. Hubbard," I greeted the ME, Boone nodding to him, too.

"Hubbs," the detective said, all casual.

"Boone, Seph, Merry Christmas." Dr. Niall Hubbard shrugged at Boone's raised eyebrow. "Not for everyone, clearly, but the sentiment is heartfelt."

"I'll get started, Hubbs." The young black

woman with him zipped up her white coverall, the hood barely containing her full, glossy curls. She hurried past me, blue booties over her shoes, heading for the balcony the two officers had carefully taped off. I was surprised Boone hadn't blocked the whole room, to be honest.

"From what Seph told me," Boone said, addressing Cherise and Trent, "there's been a lot of traffic in and out of here tonight. Forensics will go over it, but we'll have to eliminate all of your DNA and fingerprints if that's the case." Had he read my mind? No, he was just really good at what he did. I needed to stop second-guessing him and let him work.

"I understand the body is in the hot tub." Dr. Hubbard blew a strawberry. "Always messes with TOD, Boone. I'll do my best. Onward." He strolled toward the balcony, whistling a Christmas carol while one of the officers smiled at him and the ME nodded pleasantly back.

"I have to call my general manager." Yuri Ellsworth shook like a willow in a storm, spinning and hurrying from the room before anyone could stop him. Boone let him go, partly because the rest of our party decided to show up at the same time as he departed, the entry to the living room suddenly crowded with people demanding answers to questions, Callie and Thalia among them.

"Mom," my daughter said, flat stare drifting over Boone before settling on me. "What did you do?"

Nice, kid. Thanks a lot. Thalia shushed her as Callie eye rolled and tossed her head. "Are you all right, Seph?"

I nodded, two EMTs making their way through the crowd, Martin trying to lead Layla away, Carla holding Melanie's arm while Angelo joined Trent, scowling at Boone.

"I'm fine," I said. "But I'm afraid our unwanted guest is not." I caught Brin's flash of vengeful rage and then shock as she realized what I was saying. "Melanie," I said. "I'm so sorry, but Gerald is dead."

CHAPTER TWELVE

She shuddered as if struck then sagged, but she didn't cry. "Thank you," she whispered.

Yeah, that didn't sound good at *all*.

"I'm happy to assist with the investigation, detective," Trent said immediately.

"As am I." Angelo nodded in time with my ex.

"Anything you need, Boone," Cherise said.

While the handsome detective at my side smiled gently at all of them. "Nice try," he said. "You all know better. So beat it." No one moved, Boone finally sighing and gesturing for his officers who joined him. "You'll be escorted back to your rooms for the time being," the detective said in about as no-nonsense a tone as I'd ever heard, "and when I'm ready to ask you questions, you'll make yourselves

70

available." He was usually a softer touch, at least as far as I knew from the one case we worked. Then again, as protests broke out, I could only imagine he had to play this one differently.

"This is ridiculous," Trent spluttered. "Use the talent available to you."

"You're a suspect, agent," Boone dropped on him point-blank, shutting up my ex. Silence followed that blunt admission, only the soft sound of Melanie sniffling punctuating the silence. "Look," Boone said, softer now, settling into that easy and casual confidence I'd seen before, "I'm just here to do a job, agents, sheriff. I'm sure whatever happened, none of you had anything to do with it." He was stroking egos, wasn't he?

It didn't work, because each of the law enforcement individuals in our small group had said the exact same thing themselves at one point or another, right?

"I'll call your supervisor," Trent said, voice shaking.

"Detective." Angelo cut off anything that might have come after, one hand on Trent's shoulder, silencing him. Sullen and unrepentant, my ex shook his head but went quiet as his fellow agent went on. "Under the circumstances, it makes sense to utilize my particular skills to your advantage." He shook his head at Trent who tried to protest. "Agent Garret will stand down as long as I'm allowed to investigate in conjunction with the Major Crimes unit."

"You're asking me to invite you into a case that's not FBI jurisdiction," Boone said with enough amusement I saw Trent flinch in anger again. Though, make no mistake, I was positive the detective's reaction had nothing to do with taking the situation lightly. To the contrary.

"I'm asking you to do a solid for fellow law enforcement," Angelo said. "The man's wedding was just ruined, and his life turned upside down. He wants to get to the bottom of this as much as you do. And while we understand," he stressed that to Trent who again burbled an attempt at a complaint, "why Agent Garret can't be directly involved, there's no reason I can't."

"Or me," Cherise said in a not-taking-no-for-an-answer tone of voice that had Boone tossing his hands.

"I guess you want in, too?" His green eyes locked on me.

"Only if you need me, detective," I said with prim professionalism.

"Fine." Boone pointed at Trent and then Melanie, both of whom stared at him, mute, though Melanie's was stunned while my ex's was rebellious. "Take the happy couple to their present living quarters. I'll be asking some questions after I speak to the ME."

The two officers did as they were bid, leading the pair away. I watched Carla glance over her shoulder before she followed and wondered at her lack of empathy. She didn't seem all that broken up over the death of the man she'd been kissing with abandon only a few hours ago. It made me wonder, since I'd seen her exiting the room on her own. Was I looking at the face of a murderer?

She met my eyes, flat gaze furious, before she spun and left. Good riddance and maybe I'd solved this case for Boone before he even had to do any work. Nothing would make me happier than to find out Carla Helland was guilty of murder.

Yes, I was a horrible person.

Dr. Hubbard had joined us, a body in a black bag being wheeled out while the stout doctor slipped back his hood, revealing his thinning hair and tall, lined forehead as he cleaned his glasses on his coverall. He squinted up at Boone, hazel eyes small in his round face while he filled the detective in, the rest of us crowding around to hear.

"From what I can see, COD is drowning," the ME said. "No outward sign of trauma, no head injury. Petechial hemorrhaging in the eyes suggests the cause is correct. Still, you know me. I'll be thorough." He waved to the young woman who'd come with him and she joined us, what looked like a keycard in a plastic bag held in one gloved hand. "Tell Boone what you found, Ms. Mutch."

"There was no sign of forced entry according to your officers," she said. "Looks like he had a key to the room."

Odd. It certainly seemed that way, but where did he get it? And what was that gold line down the middle? I checked mine but it didn't have one. "It's not to this hotel."

"It is." Brin poked her nose in, Boone not making her leave just yet, though that was coming, I was sure. She pointed at the stripe before hugging herself. "I used to work housekeeping in a place like this. That's a maid's master."

Well, now.

"Thank you, Miss..?" Boone waited for her to answer.

"Brin Anderson," she said with sullen acceptance.

"Ah," Boone said. "Cleary?" He motioned to another officer who had just entered. "Miss Anderson needs to exit, please. Make sure she's kept apart from her mother."

Brin shot him an angry look on her way out but didn't fight or protest further as Boone turned to the forensics tech.

"Thanks, Ray," he said. "Where did you find it?"

"Floating in the hot tub," she said, sliding the bag into the silver case at her side. "I'm going to do a full sweep of the suite now, if that's okay." It was a question but didn't sound like one, more like she was going to do it regardless of his agreement or not.

"Of course." Boone herded us all out, Cherise pausing to speak to Martin and Layla while Callie pulled me aside.

"Dad didn't kill anyone," she huffed.

"Go back to our room and get some rest," I said in lieu of arguing. Because I really didn't know, did I?

"Mom." Callie tsked softly while Thalia interrupted, arm around her girlfriend's shoulders, guiding her gently away.

"I'll take care of her," she said, my daughter throwing me a furious look over her shoulder but going with Thalia, the pair disappearing behind our suite door. And don't think I wasn't acutely aware of the fact Callie's final glare was aimed at Boone.

Yeah, there was a fight ahead. Just let me get through the murder thing first, okay?

CHAPTER THIRTEEN

I woke early, feeling like I'd barely laid my head on the pillow, confirming my mere three hours sleep with a glance at my phone. But now that I was awake, there was no way to go back to rest, so I grabbed a hasty shower and hurried to return to Boone's room the next floor down.

I found him pouring over notes, welcoming me in when I used the key he'd given me and joined him on the sofa in the smaller suite he'd rented for the duration of his stay. I'd considered napping here in his room but for the sake of Callie's unhappiness and the need to focus on the case, I chose instead to distance myself somewhat from the handsome detective. At least, that had been the plan. The moment I sat next to him, our thighs touching, I felt that same wave of attraction I always did and had to catch my breath a little before I did something untoward and that would either get me booted from his room for being a distraction or end in the two of us doing something that would only complicate matters.

Boone didn't comment, though I noted he made no move to shift away from me, leaning back and linking his fingers together, hands behind his head as he watched me pour a cup of coffee.

"I finished the interviews," he said.

"Interrogations," I corrected him. "Say it like you mean it, Boone."

He chuckled but didn't argue. "If your timeline is right—and I have no reason to doubt," he sat forward again, waving off any attempt I might make to defend my memory, "it sounds like Ms. Gannister's manservant was the last person in the room around TOD."

"He doesn't give me the impression that he'd shirk at murder," I said, "but there was nothing about the way he came out of the room that suggested he'd done the deed." His arms had been dry, for one, so if he'd drowned Gerald Berman, he'd have had to have shed his jacket first. That being said, I'd seen Trent exit in his street clothes. Could he have gotten his tux wet and that was why he changed when no one else seemed to have? Okay, I had, and the girls. So, it was just Brin and Melanie who hadn't.

And neither had long sleeves. Easy enough to wipe water away.

A knock at the door had Boone on his feet, answering it. The hotel's general manager, Kate Nimitz, entered in a rush, the young maid from yesterday on her heels, looking even more downcast and upset. It probably didn't help that Yuri Ellsworth followed behind her, the night manager still present and clearly upset with her and I realized only then the poor thing was having a terrible holiday herself.

"This is Cyndi Milo," Kate said, huffing as she looked down at the cowering maid. "Apparently, she misplaced her keycard yesterday."

"It was stolen, ma'am," Cyndi squeaked. "I reported it."

"Then why is there no report?" Kate turned to Yuri who shook his head, though there was something about the way he refused to look at the maid that had me frowning.

And her gaping. "But sir," she said, "I told you my key was stolen."

"If you did," he clipped at her, "there is no record, and I don't recall it. You are responsible for your master key, Miss Milo, as you well know. The safety and security of our guests depends on your integrity. Kate, it's obvious we've misplaced our trust in this case."

"So it seems," the general manager said, shaking her head at Boone. "I'm sorry, detective."

"A moment," he said, smiling down at the weeping maid. "Miss Milo, I'm Kellan. Can you tell me exactly what happened?"

She choked off her tears and gathered herself

enough to nod. "I was cleaning on the second floor," she said, "and had just finished with 203 and opened the door to 205. This man comes stumbling toward me and falls." She held out her trembling hands like she was going to catch him all over again. "He apologized then hurried away. It wasn't until I locked up and moved on to 207 that I realized my key was gone." She looked back and forth between Boone and her general manager, pleading with them with just her expression. "You have to believe me. I take my job very seriously."

I believed her. "Can you describe the man, Miss Milo?" I wasn't taking bets on who it had been because that would be too easy.

"He was medium height and build," she said directly to me, a flicker of hope on her face as she read my empathetic reaction correctly, "bit of a scruff beard, brown hair." Sounded like Gerald Berman to me. "He smelled like alcohol." She wrinkled her nose, sniffling and wiping her own on the corner of her apron. "I told you, Mr. Ellsworth. I went right to you because I couldn't get inside to finish my floor." Panic had returned while the general manager turned to her night supervisor.

Yuri shrugged uncomfortably, but it was clear who was lying here. "Did you fill out a report?"

"You told me to go back to work," she said in a small voice, but stood her ground, bless her.

"Yuri?" The general manager's frown deepened. "What's going on?"

He suddenly paled and shook his head, backing up a step and looking down. "I want a lawyer," he said.

Well, now.

"The only reason you'd need a lawyer," Boone said in a soft voice, "is if you did something wrong, Mr. Ellsworth." The man started to tremble, licking his lips, eyes now wide and a little wild. "Why didn't you report it?"

Any nefarious reasoning connected to the case went out the window when he cracked like a bad egg. "I had a perfect sheet this month!" His wail made my teeth ache. "I earned that bonus, and you ruined it." He snarled at the maid who cowered away from him. "It's not fair."

"I'm very disappointed," Kate said, gesturing for the door. "Both of you, my office, now. Detective, my apologies." She paused a moment, regret passing over her face. "No luck yet, Ms. Pringle, but we're still looking for Belladonna."

"Thank you," I said.

"And for your assistance, Ms. Nimitz," Boone said then, escorting them out before turning to me. "So, now we know for sure where Mr. Berman got the key."

I was grateful for the return of attention to the case since worrying about my cat was getting me nowhere.

"Likely to trash the suite, and probably with Carla's assistance," I agreed. I'd filled Boone in on everything I could think of before crashing earlier, including sharing the photos I'd taken of the kissing couple. "That being said, did Carla have motive to kill Gerald? She didn't seem all that broken up by his death."

Boone headed back to the couch, and I rejoined him, sipping my coffee and trying to shake off the weariness that two nights of little sleep left me the victim of. "I'm looking into her and Mr. Berman," Boone said. "So far, nothing."

"And Stella Gannister?" I hated to think the clever and funny old woman had anything to do with this, but I knew better than to discount her for her age.

"The Gannisters have their history with state police," he said with enough enigmatic coyness I almost poked him for more, but he was pushing on himself. "And, from what I understand, the FBI as well. If Carla Helland didn't drown him, someone must have found Mr. Berman in the suite and done the deed." He hesitated before I shrugged.

"I know Trent's on the list," I said.

"And Melanie Anderson, her daughter, Brin." He nodded. "Sorry, Seph."

"Just prove Carla Helland did it," I said, "and you'll make my Christmas."

"I get you're not a fan," Boone said, "but you can't just arrest people willy-nilly for being terrible human beings, Seph. Or our prison system would be in way worse trouble than it already is."

"A girl can dream," I said, setting aside my coffee, noticing a photo on the coffee table of what looked like a cell in plastic. "What's that?"

"Mr. Berman's phone," he said, holding it up. "Rachel says it's mostly ruined, the water and heat got to it. But she's doing her best to see if there's anything salvageable. I'm not holding my breath." He set the image down, selecting another paper, this one with the ME's signature on it. "Hubbs narrowed TOD to between 9 and 11PM, but that was the best he could do. He said the legs being out of the water in cold air as opposed to the rest under hot water messed up his ability to predict perfectly, so we have a definite two-hour window of frustration."

The same window in which I'd seen each of the suspects near the bridal suite. Excellent and most unhelpful.

"I need to ask you to step off, Seph." Boone's request came as a huge shock. I stared at him, took in his wince, his heavy sigh and the way one hand settled on my knee while those green eyes pleaded with me. "I know, okay? It's not that I don't trust you. But you're too close to this and we both know it."

"Like I wasn't too close to Thalia's case," I said. No, snapped, because yeah, I was tired, and he just had to poke the bear after everything I'd been through.

"I get that," he said so carefully I pulled away.

"Don't try to handle me, Boone." He stayed seated as I stood and took a few steps away. "It's insulting and I deserve better."

"You certainly don't deserve to find another body and have to defend your ex and his fiancé," Boone said without a hint of judgment. "Seph, please. Let me take care of this. He's law enforcement, and not just local. I've got the feds breathing down my neck, my supervisor backing me up, for now, but this could turn into a real crap show, and I don't want it to…" he trailed off, paused a long moment.

Boone didn't have to finish. "You don't want it to hurt our relationship," I said, flat and frustrated. "Except asking me to step aside will, Boone. Trust me on that."

He didn't say a word, didn't nod or move a muscle, just watched me with his careful gaze and a calm, soothing expression devoid of anything challenging. Which only made things worse, because maybe if he'd fought with me I could have vented this horrible knot of awful that had suddenly taken up residence in my stomach.

"The truth of the matter is," Boone said then, tone still soft and calm but words cutting through his compassion, "there's an excellent chance either Trent Garret, Melanie or Brin Anderson murdered Gerald Berman. Possibly together." Wait, what? "I'd hate to see it come between us," he finished so quietly I had to strain to hear him, "but if it does, so be it, Seph. I have to do my job. And I want you out of it."

There wasn't much I could say to that. Instead of tossing out something mean and hurtful, however, a cruelty I didn't intend and would forever regret, I chose to retreat with my head high and my anger bubbling.

All the way to the door and out of it, closing it behind me. Only to find Angelo and Cherise on the other side, scowling and visibly hungry and eager as I approached.

"Kicked you out, too?" My sheriff friend's growl sounded feral.

"Just let him try," Angelo snarled.

Not hard to make the right decision, was it? Kellen Boone be damned.

"Let's get to work," I said. And told them everything I knew.

CHAPTER FOURTEEN

We ended up in Angelo's room, next door to Trent's new one.

"The detective has him sequestered," my husband's partner said.

"Angelo." I confronted him, not wanting any secrets between us and remembering what I'd seen the night before, "why were you talking to the victim in the lobby?" I'd assumed Angelo was confronting Gerald about stopping the wedding, but could there have been more to it?

He hesitated, frowning, something dark crossing his face before he lightened up again and nodded. "I went after him," he said. "Of course, I did. Someone had to." Fair enough. "The jerk spilled his drink on my tux, got the sleeve all wet, laughed about it." He shrugged then. "It took everything I had not to beat the crap out of him."

Phew, okay. "So, if I looked at your shirt from last night," I said, recalling the second point that had me nervous, "it would be stained with champagne?"

Angelo stared at me for a long time while Cherise prodded me.

"Seph, Angelo had no reason to kill Gerald," she said.

"I know that," I told her. "But we have to eliminate one another." They both nodded immediately. "Due diligence in this case, if only for Trent and Melanie. Agreed?" Another pair of matching nods. "Well?" I pointed at his right arm. "You had your coat draped when I ran into you. If your arm was wet from drowning someone, it would be a great way to hide it."

Angelo spun and went to the garment bag hanging over the back of the sofa, unzipping it and pulling out his white shirt. There was a definite stain from the fabric being wet, but a single sniff identified the source as alcoholic in nature, though I did catch a faint whiff of chlorine. Which, I realized as my suspicious mind relented, could be attributed to bleach at the cleaners.

"Okay," I said, turning to Cherise this time as she stared me down like a perfectly carved statue of a goddess of war ready to do battle in her jeans and short jacket. "You are Trent's best friend," I said. "Your room was right down the hall, and you had easy access if you decided to ask him for his key."

She nodded. "Except my husband and kid can

tell you I never left the suite after we all left around 6:30," she said. "We had a quiet dinner, like I know you did because I saw the delivery at the same time mine arrived, then retired to watch movies and try to forget the mess. I fell asleep and only came out when I heard voices in the hallway."

That was a relief. Not that I believed it of her, but I had to ask.

Which meant they now faced me down with serious expressions while I inhaled and slowly exhaled before lifting my chin.

"I found the body," I said, "and I was in the room with no good reason to be there." Neither of them said a word, letting me go on. I told them everything I'd witnessed, from Melanie and Trent's argument and subsequent parting of ways, how I'd seen Brin hurrying away, then Angelo, followed by my sighting of Carla leaving the room before Trent went in and out and, finally, the mysterious Stella Gannister.

Angelo seemed agitated at that. "What's she doing here?"

"You know her?" Maybe some answers were finally forthcoming.

"Later," he said, all focused FBI agent. "You said you had photographic proof of the affair?"

I showed them the images I'd taken, Cherise's anger sparking as her full lips narrowed into a thin, furious line.

"You should have told me," she said.

"Right," I shot back, "so we'd have two murders to investigate." She tsked at me but I faced her down.

87

"Cherise, it wouldn't have served anyone to tell them about it last night. Bad enough everything that did happen, let alone hurting Melanie further."

"Except there's a chance Melanie did find out," Angelo said.

"But why kill Gerald if that's the case?" I'd have targeted Carla.

"Maybe she was next on the list, and he made himself an easy first target." What did that mean? Angelo hesitated then sighed. "Look, I have a friend at the state lab who owes me. They called him in, so he's pissed and told me just out of spite. Gerald Berman's blood alcohol was 0.25." Cherise whistled sharply while I cocked an eyebrow for clarification. "If he wasn't out cold, he was on the brink of it and more than likely was suffering from alcohol poisoning."

"Could it have been an accident?" That had never crossed my mind, though it did with a flicker of relief. "Maybe he trashed the room, got drunk and fell in the tub."

"If that's true," Cherise said, "this might be over sooner than later."

"I hear Boone's a stickler for every detail," Angelo said, pacing a little. "Not that I blame him, in fact I applaud his tenacity. If it was an accident, he'll figure it out."

"So, we wait, then," Cherise said. "To hear what Hubbs says." She knew the ME? Of course, she did.

"A bit of clandestine digging won't hurt in the meantime," Angelo said, gaze meeting mine. "Up for it?"

"You better believe it." Because I was not leaving the safety of my ex and his soon-to-be-wife to the possibility that Boone found the truth.

I trusted him, yes. But he was still a cop with an agenda, well-intentioned or not.

"I say we part ways," Angelo said. "From what Trent says, you have your own way of doing things, Cherise." The sheriff nodded while the FBI agent turned to me with a wry grin. "And I understand you're just as bad."

"Guilty," I said. "We check in on regular intervals or if we find out anything and compare notes, agreed?" They both nodded instantly, Cherise beating me to the door.

"Don't do anything overt," Angelo called after us.

Which made Cherise snort and wink at me. "Hear that, Seph?"

"Good luck with that," I muttered under my breath. Angelo didn't know it yet, but he'd just let the bull loose in the china shop and she wasn't holding back.

Though, first? I had some digging to do, and my laptop wasn't going to boot itself.

CHAPTER FIFTEEN

I sent the girls skiing when they tried to linger, shooing them out of the suite and setting myself up with a carafe of coffee and a kick-ass internet connection that had me whipping through the suspects in short order.

First, I looked into the victim, however, checking for any connection he might have had to Carla outside his marriage to Melanie. It was pretty apparent to me as I scrolled through mentions of him on the search engine that he'd been arrested multiple times for grifting and cons, though he'd never served any serious time. His social media presence was almost non-existent, however, so there was no way to look into his background further past the newspaper articles and occasional press releases from the police department, so I finally had to let the dead man lie.

Carla was next and I couldn't wait to uncover dirt on her, though what I had was already sufficient, I believed, to at least get her out of Melanie's life forever—and, in turn, mine, which suited me just fine. My desire to prove the woman had committed murder hadn't waned, though I was honest enough with myself that when I caught moments of trying to mush findings together into a cohesive whole when it came to Gerald, I purposely tore them apart again and had to reluctantly admit there was no proof she knew him with any physical intimacy prior to the wedding.

No proof, no. But they knew each other, that much was obvious due to her proximity to Melanie and that woman's marriage to the victim. So, either they'd never been overt, or they'd never been caught, and that just made them all the more disgusting to me. And encouraged my mind to weave Carla into the murderous narrative I was hoping for.

Now, you might think I was awful for wanting it to be her, but I had ulterior motives. First, if she did it, that meant Trent didn't and my daughter wouldn't have to visit her father in prison instead of at his FBI office. And second, if Carla was the killer, that meant my ex wouldn't be crushed and heartbroken by the fact his fiancé was a murderer and that he was forced to put her away for killing her husband just to marry Trent.

Lots of good reasons, thank you. Never mind the satisfaction of seeing the adulterer of attitude behind bars where she belonged.

The sound of voices outside my door drew me away from the computer and to the peephole, those same voices now raised as I spotted Melanie in the corridor and instantly pulled the door open to see what was going on. I wasn't as surprised as I could have been to see her spinning from Stella Gannister's door and heading the other way, the old woman quietly watching her go. I immediately exited to the hall and joined Stella who looked up at me with a soft, sad smile.

"Persephone," she said, as though unsurprised by my arrival, almost seeming to expect it, in fact, "how lovely to see you. Please, come in." She stepped back, cane nowhere in evidence and, taking a chance, I did as I was bid.

Domino stood near the sofa of the cookie-cutter living room to my own, waiting for his mistress to return, faint distress on his face, though he didn't seem to be aiming it at me.

"Sit, please," Stella said, using my arm for support. I guided her to the couch and sat next to her, noting Domino's twitch as though he fought off the urge to replace me as her guide. "Tea?"

I accepted a cup, though I didn't drink it, giving her a pointed look as she dropped two cubes of sugar into her own and set off a tinkling song with the small silver spoon that she used to stir.

"We didn't meet by chance," I said.

"I never said we did," she replied, a dollop of cream following her sugar. She stirred again, the porcelain cup ringing from the attention before she sat back and sipped. "They do have fine tea in this place," she said.

"Stella." I sighed deeply, setting my cup aside on its saucer, not in the mood for games, "you're neck deep in this. I saw you talking to the dead man Christmas Eve. And I saw you and Domino at the bridal suite last night." I pointed at her bodyguard who didn't even acknowledge I'd spoken about him. "I watched him go in the room. Do you have reason to want Gerald Berman dead?"

Stella rested her cup on the saucer, eyes unreadable. "Family business," she said, confirming what I suspected.

"Melanie," I said.

She shrugged with great grace, offering me a plate. "Cookie?"

It was clear she had no intention of telling me anything, but I couldn't just let this go. The thing was, I wasn't given a choice, not when someone knocked, and Domino moved to answer. Imagine Boone's surprise when he found me having tea with Stella Gannister? Though, surprise wasn't the expression he wore, was it? I think disappointment was much more the flavor of the hour.

"I'm so sorry, my dear," Stella said before Boone could say a word. "I was so sure I heard Bella crying. Such a shame she's still missing. If I hear her again, I'll let you know." She handed me a slip of paper. "My number, just in case you need to reach me."

The old fox. She'd covered for me. I nodded stiffly and stood, taking her card. "Thank you," I said, turning to Boone whose lips had narrowed, eyes, too, but that frustration was gone so if he knew of the subterfuge, he didn't argue with it. "Detective," I said, and breezed out past him, giving Domino the stink-eye on the way by.

Probably not the smartest thing to do, being saucy with someone who was obviously trained to kill with his bare hands, but I was in that kind of mood.

Drama wrapped up for the moment, I took a moment to enter Stella's number into my phone before I returned to my laptop and this time did a deep dive on Melanie. Yes, I'd looked into her before, of course, I had. She wasn't just marrying Trent, she was going to be Callie's stepmom and that was more important to me than her matrimonial plans. But, like every other time (stop, no judging) I'd peeked, Melanie's social media and background seemed impeccable. Mind you, from what I could tell, she struggled with her business and with debt, but other than that, she seemed perfectly ordinary.

Not ordinary, though, was she?

As for Brin, she'd had her own troubles with the police, though unlike her father, hers were mostly nuisance issues like drunk and disorderly and being arrested for possession. Pretty innocent teenager/early twenties stuff that, while not ideal, weren't exactly putting her in the killer rampage category.

I had to look into the Gannister family, naturally who, it turned out, were much like the Vesterville's only on the downside of their original wealth. There were enough stories in financial magazines about the fall of some of their family corporations that it was clear to me Stella was hanging onto her position with grit and determination. And, more than likely, more than a little criminal activity if the insider trading that got her nephew, Hylan Gannister, arrested for securities fraud, revealed anything.

I'd almost abandoned that trail when I spotted what I'd been looking for. An old family photo of the whole clan from about thirty years prior. And while she was very young in the image, I was positive the girl beside Stella was none other than Melanie Anderson.

But why keep her connection to the Gannister family a secret? Unless she had something to be ashamed of. Or didn't want her soon-to-be FBI husband to know. Sketchy.

Domino was a dead end because without a last name, there wasn't much I could dig up. I did manage to find a photo of him with Stella, but an internet search of his face turned up squat. Hardly a surprise. People like him were as invisible as they came and proving he killed Gerald might just mean this case went unsolved if he actually did the deed.

That would be worst case scenario right after Trent, Melanie or Brin being convicted because I knew what something like this hanging over my ex's head would do to him.

And while I knew I could trust him, I ran a check on SSA Angelo Flores anyway, just in case. Turns out he was not only a decorated agent, he was an adrenaline junkie, into freeclimbing, base jumping, motorcycle racing and more. I took one look at the video he'd made of a base jump he'd done a few months ago and turned it off with a shudder. There were lots of stupid ways to die and he, apparently, wanted to master all of them before one of them ended his life.

Well, good on him, if that was what made him happy. I was about to shut down that line of inquiry when a last name caught my eye. Because who was it do you think arrested Hylan Gannister for fraud?

None other than SSA Angelo Flores.

Now, wasn't *that* interesting.

CHAPTER SIXTEEN

He'd lied to me. To my face. And that had my back up. All he had to do was say so, right? Which meant he was hiding something, and I needed to know what.

I went on a hunt that paid off for me almost immediately. Running into Angelo on the elevator while just setting out to find him meant he had the full force of my impending doom to deal with. His surprised expression at my grim one only increased when I took full advantage of the situation and pressed the stop button to have a private moment. That made the small box we found ourselves in a very tense place to be. After all, I might have known some judo and been in decent shape, but Angelo was a trained agent and a risk-junkie. I knew I didn't stand a chance if he came at me.

Didn't stop me from poking him in the chest with an accusatory finger, though. "You said you didn't know Gerald Berman," I snapped.

He shook his head, scowling. "What's this about?"

"Hylan Gannister," I said and watched understanding cross the agent's face.

"What about him?" This was no time to be cagey and I let him know it.

"Melanie is a Gannister," I said. "Isn't she?"

Angelo's attempt to deny ended in a deep sigh when I crossed my arms over my chest and waited him out.

"Yes," he said, very softly and with regret, dark eyes now sad. "Or she was. She disowned the family years ago."

"You knew," I said. "Did Trent?"

"No." Regret hung in that single word. "Seph, I couldn't say anything. It was a case." He shook his head, tossing his hands. "I know, I should have. But by the time I reconnected with Trent, he was already engaged to Melanie. How was I supposed to tell him the love of his life was a cousin to a man I put away for fraud? And that the rest of them are under continual investigation?"

Well, okay then. Considering the fact that I'd held off on sharing the Carla tidbit, I guess I could understand. And a lot could be explained about Angelo's secrecy when it came to the FBI and official need-to-know. But we were past that now and I needed to know.

"No more secrets," I said. "Were you looking into Gerald?"

"To the contrary," Angelo said before pausing then submitting at last. "I could lose my job for this, Seph."

Wait. "He was your CI." Confidential informant, and thus sacrosanct in law enforcement. No wonder Angelo lied. His lack of reaction told me everything. And had me pressing the start button on the elevator again. "I get it," I said. "You really need to tell Boone."

"It's an ongoing case," Angelo said. "I can't say anything to anyone."

"Your CI is dead," I said as the doors opened and delivered us to the lobby.

"Maybe so," he said, still skirting the truth, "but that doesn't mean the case is."

"You're with the crazy killer squad now," I said, knowing Trent would hate that I called his division that, serials only a part of what he did, albeit a big part.

"Every agent has a case they can't let go of," Angelo said, hands in his pockets, frowning more deeply, clearly agitated as he shuffled his feet as if eager to go. "I still have a vested interest in seeing the Gannister family face the justice they deserve."

"Did you know Gerald was going to show up and ruin everything?" I saw the denial in Angelo immediately, his horror at the idea authentic.

"I'd have made sure he didn't if I had," the agent told me with some heat before calming again. "Trent is my friend, Seph. And he's not a murderer."

I wished we could agree on that because I still wasn't positive and hated myself for it.

We parted ways without further conversation while I debated telling Boone what Angelo had been up to. While it wasn't pertinent to the murder on the surface, what if the Gannisters found out Gerald was a rat and had him killed? Domino certainly had the physique and wherewithal. But his headshake as he exited the room and Stella's obvious frustration lingered with me. Neither of them had the look of people happy with the end result of murder. Instead, they'd both seemed disappointed in something.

Rather than make the decision right away, I returned to the suites and knocked on Carla's door. I had prepared myself to push my way into the room, not to take no for an answer from the nasty woman I now knew betrayed Melanie (and maybe in more ways than one) only to have Brin open the way and welcome me inside immediately.

She hugged me as soon as she closed the door, and I embraced her back. When she let me go, her eyes brimmed with tears. "Thanks for checking in," she said.

"You might not be so happy I'm here in a minute." I turned to Melanie who had curled up on a corner of the couch with a box of tissues and a blanket. "I have to ask your mother some hard questions."

"Ask," Melanie croaked, voice hoarse, likely from all her crying and more pending. "I have nothing to hide from anyone."

I joined her on the sofa, Brin sitting on the coffee

table facing us both, while I took Melanie's free hand. "You're a Gannister," I said.

She coughed softly, nodding. "You're so clever," she said. "I knew you'd figure it out. Yes, my mother was. I took my father's last name even though my grandmother disapproved. Right before I left the family."

"Stella Gannister," I said. Melanie nodded again while Brin just listened. Had they had this conversation themselves already? Possibly, though from the intensity of the younger Anderson's attention, maybe she was hoping for more than she'd been able to glean from her mother. "She's your grandmother. And the source, I presume, of the inheritance Gerald was suing you for."

Melanie straightened a little but stared down at her hands and the tissue she was picking apart a small piece at a time, her perfectly manicured nails ragged around the edges from anxious nibbling. "I wanted nothing to do with the Gannister fortune," she said. "Or my trust fund. Grandmother set it up for me, but I never touched it, and I never will." Her eyes met mine with sincerity and sorrow. "Nothing good ever came from that family, Seph." I'd heard that before. What was it about old money that ruined lives so very deeply? "That's why when my father died, I took Brin and ran."

"Why didn't you tell me?" Her daughter's anger surfaced again, though Brin seemed to do her best to suppress the bulk of it. "You could have, Mom." *Should have* was also implied.

"I was trying to protect you," Melanie said, voice

now low and trembling, not meeting Brin's eyes. "I was a fool. Grandmother reached out when she heard about the wedding. She's been spying on me all these years. She wanted to come, and I said no."

"Apparently Stella Gannister doesn't take no for an answer," I said.

"She accepted my decision all those years ago," Melanie told me, "but with cousin Hylan in prison and the rest of the family under constant scrutiny, I think she's feeling isolated. She said she just wanted her family back together." Melanie sniffled, wiping her nose with a fresh tissue. "I should have told Trent, but I thought I could maintain what I'd done. Grandmother won't live forever." She shuddered, her own anger showing in her face when she looked up again. "She must have told Gerald. It's the only reason he'd have shown up here."

"You didn't exactly keep it a secret, Mom," Brin said. "It was all over your social." She shook her head like her mother had no idea how easy it was to track such activity if someone wanted to keep tabs on you. Was Melanie really that innocent?

But her mother's scowl didn't fade. "I wouldn't put it past Grandmother to set this up to ruin everything." Not innocent, then, but in a blame cycle as old as she likely was and unable to see the forest for the trees. Fair enough.

"You may have this backwards," I said to Melanie as my mind worked through the idea. "If she thought him a threat to your happiness, would your grandmother have Gerald killed to protect you?"

Melanie seemed startled by that, blinking and

obviously taking a moment to think about it before she sighed deeply, more tears rising in her eyes as her lips twisted against her need to sob. "Oh my god," she whispered. "Maybe."

Someone knocked on the door, Brin rising without hesitation to answer it while Melanie's mind visibly scrolled through the suggested scenario, each change of emotion and awareness showing on her face.

"You know what," she finally said to me, wonder and amazement replacing sorrow, "you might be right. She might have had him killed for me. She always hated him."

"As much as I would love to claim the end result," Stella's voice interrupted, Melanie and I both looking up, startled at her appearance, "hypothetically, of course," she winked at me, "I'm afraid neither I nor my faithful manservant had a thing to do with the death of Gerald Berman. Though I have raised a glass of sherry to his memory." She sat in the stuffed chair at the end of the sofa without being asked, silver cane tucked between her ankles as Domino came to stand behind her in looming support. Brin stood back, eyes huge as she took in her great-grandmother and the conversation unfolding, until Stella looked up at her and smiled so kindly and with such welcome that I caught Brin's tremor of response. "Come, dear one," Stella said, hand reaching out, "and say hello to your great-grandmother."

I suppose I shouldn't have been surprised when Brin moved immediately to do so, nor by the visible discomfort on Melanie's face to see her daughter kneel to hug the woman she'd fled from when Brin was a baby. No, my surprise came by how moved I felt.

Whose side was I on, anyway?

CHAPTER SEVENTEEN

My phone vibrated, pulling me away from the family drama as I stood to stride to the fireplace to check it.

TOD finally narrowed down to 11PM, Boone sent. Which meant everyone had been in and out after Gerald Berman died. Great, that helped not even a little. *He had a lot of alcohol in his system.* Whoops, already knew that, thanks, Boone. *But Hubbs says not an accident, fibers found under the victim's nails and Rachel found sequins on the bottom of the pool.* Huh, Carla had been wearing that gaudy and highly inappropriate dress. Didn't it have sequins?

What color? I fired off that question as I noted Melanie hadn't moved, though Stella was in quiet conversation with Brin. I was surprised Trent's fiancé didn't attempt to stop the pair from talking but either the fight had gone out of Melanie, or she'd changed her mind about her family. Whatever the case, Stella didn't look threatening in any way and Brin was a grown woman, so I left them to carry on as Boone responded.

White, he sent.

Carla Helland, I sent back. And yes, with a smirk. So there.

My thoughts exactly. I'm going to arrange to see the footage on your floor shortly. Want to come?

Nice of you to offer, I sent. *Meet you in the lobby.*

Fifteen minutes, he sent.

Perfect timing. Though I had this little tête-à-tête to wrap up first.

"I'm a bit insulted you took advantage of me Christmas Eve.." I did nothing to keep the cynical amusement from my voice, Stella looking up from Brin who'd crouched at her feet for their talk. The old woman's matching wry grin told the story.

"Now, my dear Persephone," Stella said. "I was looking for information and you presented yourself perfectly."

"You could have just told me instead of playing me like that." Maybe I should have felt a bit grumpier about the whole thing, but she really was clever and despite whatever illegal things she and her family had been up to, I continued to feel a begrudging admiration and, yes, I admit it, open liking for Stella Gannister.

"You swear to me you didn't have Domino kill Gerald." I already knew otherwise, but I wanted to hear her say it.

Stella laughed out loud, even the hulking bodyguard flashing the barest smile at me. "My dear," the old woman said, "if I ever considered anything of the sort, I certainly wouldn't be foolish enough to leave any evidence behind." She winked. "Hypothetically." Okay then. Stella sobered somewhat, leaning on her cane with one hand, the other touching Brin's cheek. "My only goal is to return my family to the fold and enjoy their company in my final days."

"You're not going anywhere soon," I said, again with a cynical edge and she shrugged, because her weakness had been all an act too and I was a sucker.

"Anything can happen, Persephone." True that. "I've wasted enough time." Stella's gaze fell to Melanie. "All I want is to reconcile. You don't have to take my money, my dear, or have anything to do with any other Gannister. But I miss you, darling Melanie, and I've so longed to get to know Brin as I never had the chance to really know Ethan."

That had to hurt. Melanie's son had died from tragic circumstances, after all. The young woman who was his sister held her great-grandmother's hand, obviously won over while Melanie still hesitated. Whatever history there was between them, it wasn't my business at the moment. I had security footage to screen with a certain gorgeous detective and that was a date I didn't plan to miss.

Even if I'd wanted to stay, as the door opened, my welcome washed up and blew away. Carla Helland took one look at me and scowled, Stella rising immediately despite Carla's focus, Domino maneuvering the old woman past the surly maid-of-honor with his large body carefully placed between them as Stella let herself out. I was surprised Brin went with her, Melanie staying behind, and followed without Carla having to kick me out, but just barely.

I did spare her a wink on the way through the door, however. I just couldn't help myself. Because for me, the footage I was about to peruse was going to seal the deal on Carla's murderous inclinations and wrap up this case lickety-split.

I was almost whistling when I got off the elevator, certainly in higher spirits than I had been since Belladonna's disappearance, so when I spotted two familiar people standing with Boone at the far end of the lobby's desk, I wasn't expecting the load of dread that hit the bottom of my stomach with a hearty thud. Way to ruin the mood, y'all. It was obvious from the detective's unhappy expression he'd discovered we'd been poking around despite his "request" to the contrary. I joined them with trepidation but my determination intact and that only seemed to aggravate Boone further.

As it turned out, however, it wasn't Cherise, Angelo and myself that had the detective riled up, the closed door to the manager's office opening quickly before I could ask the obvious, Kate Nimitz emerging with flushed cheeks and a dreadful look on her face.

"I'm afraid I've confirmed it, Detective Boone," she said. "Someone has erased all of the footage from the suites, all floors, all accesses, for the two hours you requested." I almost felt sorry for her. She was having a very bad few days, what with Bella's disappearance, her maid's key theft, a murder, a ruined event and now this. She must have hated to see us coming. "Your forensics person called and is on her way, but I don't know what else I can do."

"Thank you, Ms. Nimitz," Boone said. "Please give Ms. Mutch free rein when she arrives and keep me posted." Kate disappeared back into her office while the detective turned to us. "Whoever erased the footage had to have the skills to break into the security room and find the correct feeds. That takes time and training."

I certainly wouldn't have known where to start, so I agreed with him. "So, the killer either had help," I said, "or specialty education." That had me glancing up at Angelo.

He shook his head, both hands out. "I'm not into tech," he said.

Boone glared back and forth between us. "Why would Seph suspect you, Agent Flores?"

And I was an idiot.

"Detective," Angelo said, then stopped. "Let's find somewhere to talk."

We took over a corner of the bar, Angelo telling both Cherise and Boone about his connection to the Gannisters.

"It's public record I was the lead agent on that arrest," Angelo said with some heat, clearly tired of defending himself. "I didn't try to hide that."

"I take it you're all going to continue to investigate unless I arrest you?" Boone waved off our protests with a sigh, unsurprised so he must have known the information Angelo shared already. "Fine, tell me what you've learned." Not above taking full advantage of our nosiness, was he?

"Not much," Cherise said, "though I did have a friend at the Bureau tell me the man working for Stella Gannister has a particular skillset."

Hardly surprising. "Let me guess," I said. "Gun for hire?"

"More like trained assassin," she said. "He's quiet, discreet and expensive."

"And if he killed Gerald Berman," I said, "he'd have done so in a way that looked like an accident or eliminated the body entirely." No one argued right away, though Boone finally did speak up.

"Unless he was interrupted." That was a possibility, while again the image of him shaking his head in frustration to Stella stuck with me.

"He was the last one I saw in the room," I said. "Sure, someone else could have gone in when I was getting a key, fair enough." What was that flicker of something on Boone's face? I ignored it as I pushed on. "But the timing is off. So, I don't think he did it." I was still holding out for Carla. "You said your tech found white sequins in the hot tub?" Cherise and Angelo both perked at that.

Boone's flat stare told me I'd overstepped but too bad. This wasn't a pissing match, it was a murder investigation and I wasn't going to let ego get in the way of solving it. "And black fibers under his fingernails," he said. "But any DNA evidence would be destroyed by the treated water, not to mention the heat."

"We do know Carla Helland was wearing a white sequin dress," Cherise said.

"And that they had a relationship." I nodded.

"What if she joined him to trash the room," Angelo said, leaning in. "Gerald was already drunk and obnoxious. They got in a fight over something, and she pushed him into the hot tub?" It made a lot of sense. "I spoke to one of the staff here at the bar. He said he saw Melanie here in that two-hour window, drinking. Carla was with her, but he said she kept leaving and coming back, at least twice. He didn't know how long she was gone, but he said it seemed like a fair amount of time and she appeared rattled the second time."

"I spoke to the same bartender," Boone said. "And checked the time on the footage. The first time, she was gone for almost a half hour. The next, only about ten minutes, right around 11PM."

"More than enough time to drown Gerald and come back," I said. "Especially with a 0.25 blood alcohol content."

Boone's gaze flattened out again. "I didn't tell you that number." The three of us stayed very quiet after that, until the detective sighed deeply one last time, big hand running over his eyes. "Whatever," he said. "There's one final detail that none of you have yet to wring out of my network." Which was? "The last key to open the lock on the door to the suite, right at 10PM, was registered to the person who checked in. So, tell me—is Special Agent in Charge Trent Garret capable of murder?"

CHAPTER EIGHTEEN

Now I knew why Boone's reaction to my comment about Domino being the last person in the room fell short. But why was it Cherise and Angelo were both solid *no ways* when it came to Trent and I was the outside *maybe* one? Both of them seemed surprised by my hesitation, though Boone wasn't.

"You have your doubts?" The detective had to put me on the spot like that.

"I know Trent," I said. "Under normal circumstances, of course not. But these aren't normal, and he's been acting out of character." I appealed to both of his friends who seemed to relent somewhat, if reluctantly. "Have you ever seen him lose it like he did at the wedding?"

The Amazonian sheriff finally shook her head

and sighed. "Never," Cherise said.

"Not once, even under the more horrific situations," Angelo admitted. They both exchanged a guilty look before sagging a bit while I hated what I just did to them.

"Look," I said, "there's one way to prove he didn't do it. We prove that Carla did."

"That's not the way this works," Boone said, though his attitude had softened somewhat, probably because we were all finally being honest about everything. "Innocent until proven guilty while following the evidence. Not targeting one person to save another."

"As long as the job gets done," I shot back, "and the guilty party goes down."

He didn't comment on my intent. "I haven't alerted Ms. Helland to the fact I'm aware of her infidelity yet. I've been investigating other avenues." In other words, he'd been focused on Trent.

"Time to poke that cheating bear in the butt," I said.

Boone's phone vibrated before he could argue with me, the text he perused making his eyebrows rise before he met all of our gazes as he shared what he'd received. "My tech managed to pull the last received text off the vic's phone," he said. "Looks like Seph might be right after all." He turned it so we could read it, though I had to lean around to skim the single line.

Meet me in the bridal suite. We have work to do.

"Whose number sent that?" Cherise asked before I could.

113

"Carla Helland's," Boone said, bumping me with his hip. "Time for a chat with the maid-of-honor."

Oh, *yeah*, baby.

Boone was already striding out ahead of me, Cherise with her head down next to Angelo. All three of them missed the sad sight of my ex hunkered down, alone and slumped forward over a glass, in another booth on the far side of the bar. I let them go, sliding in across from Trent who barely looked up, downing his drink and accepting the next one from the waitress who I sent away without ordering anything.

He was drinking more than enough for the both of us, straight whiskey from the smell, neat and taken in mouthfuls. Another aberrant bit of behavior that had me worried. Trent never overindulged. I had to slide over when Cherise joined us, the tall sheriff taking the glass from Trent's hand, but not before he drained this one, too.

I'd never seen my ex drunk, not once in the years we'd known one another. His utter control and self-discipline never allowed for it. It was one of the many things he'd judged me for with his careful looks and subtle comments that were on the list of items of note that ended our relationship. Seeing him so desolate and despondent, unshaven with his hair a mess, eyes watery and red, a stain on the front of his sweater that he'd normally have found abhorrent, I could only think the absolute worst.

What else would drive someone like Trent Garret to such depths but guilt over something so against his nature it cracked him in half?

"I didn't kill that man." Did he know what I was thinking? He always seemed capable of reading my mind, another checkmark against us. His analytical brain and oh-so-cleverly and carefully nurtured talent at seeing the darkest parts of people had bled over into our personal lives, no matter how hard he tried to keep work at the office. So, despite his drunken state, he retained that ability, I guess, though it had to have been on his own thoughts, right?

"We know, Trent," Cherise said, turning to meet my eyes and waiting for me to back her up. I did so with a murmur, weak but present.

Trent spoke again as if he hadn't heard us. "Did you see what he did?" He wavered there, a single tear falling from his eye to the table, splashing as it hit. "Our room, our wedding, all of it. Did you see?" His hazel eyes implored both of us, sudden dismay at his empty glass driving him back and raising his arm to motion for the waitress. I had no intention of allowing him any more to drink and Cherise seemed of the same mind, whispering "water and coffee" to the server who quickly nodded in sympathy and hurried off. "He ruined everything. But I didn't kill him. I'm glad he's dead, though." Trent sighed softly, a resigned little sound that had my heart breaking for him all over again. "That makes me a bad person." I opened my mouth to argue only for him to ramble onward. "I should have made sure she checked." He slurred part of that, but I sussed enough to know what he meant, clarified by his next words. "But I love her, you know?" Again with that sad little exhale

115

of acceptance and resignation. "I wanted to believe her. There's so much she didn't tell me." He sat back again when the server set a coffee in front of him, a tall glass of water dripping condensation onto the tabletop. Trent didn't protest the lack of alcohol, helping himself to the mug and cupping it in his hands as he stared bleakly into the dark depths. "Some FBI agent I am."

"Trent." I laid one hand on his wrist, leaning forward and squeezing so he'd look up, which he did. Was he going to hear a word I said? I wasn't sure, but I was damned well going to try. "We all have blind spots when it comes to the people we love. You're an amazing investigator with a brilliant track record. When your heart is involved, it's easy to turn a blind eye. You know that. You've encountered it through your whole career, with suspects and victims."

He bobbed a half-hearted nod. "I could have done it." He blurted that while Cherise and I sat very still, almost as one, both of us locked onto him as he sipped his coffee like he hadn't just come this close to admitting to murder. "I wish I had," he whispered. Sobbed once, sagging forward, mouth open as though unable to breathe. Cherise slipped over to the other side of the table, her arm around his shoulders, dark eyes asking me to give him space.

Which I did, as much as I wanted to stay and try to help. Because he wasn't in a place of accepting it right now, not even close. He needed a friend, not his ex-wife with all the baggage we had making things worse. One thing was sure to me, however, and it lifted my spirits despite the fact he crumbled into Cherise like a broken child needing comfort.

Trent did not kill Gerald Berman.

Amen and halleluiah.

I caught up with Boone at Carla's suite, walking through the door that had been left open, lured there by the sound of shrieking. She was clearly taking his line of questioning well, barely coherent as I slipped inside and stood behind the detective. There was no sign of Angelo, wherever the agent had gotten to, but I was more interested in the relaxed stance Boone had adopted, the way Melanie stared with huge eyes at Carla who raged and rampaged in pacing fury across the carpet and realized I'd arrived just in time for the fun and fireworks.

Awesome.

The only downside? Callie and Thalia were present, huddling next to Melanie, my daughter's protective nature showing on her face as belligerence toward the detective flashed deep and angry. Even Thalia looked furious and while the two of them had a bit of history with Boone themselves, I'd hoped Callie wouldn't hold a grudge since I was dating the man.

Guess that was too much to ask for.

"Leave Melanie alone," my daughter said when Carla drew a breath between bouts of "lawyer" and "leave immediately" to give Calliope space to speak.

"You heard her," Thalia said. "She wants a lawyer."

"Actually," Boone replied to the pair of them, ignoring Carla and focusing on the stunned and wounded woman on the sofa, "Ms. Anderson hasn't made that request." He finally acknowledged Carla. "Not directly."

The maid-of-dishonor spun on Melanie and practically spit at her. "Lawyer up, you idiot!"

Melanie shook her head, still mute but either unable or unwilling to do so. I recognized the signs of deep shock, that she'd retreated further into herself, the weeping done, likely triggered by her grandmother's appearance and her subsequent time with Carla who no doubt took advantage of Melanie's delicate state.

Time to snap her out of it before her so-called friend got her sent to prison for murder.

"Melanie," I snapped, "why did you kill Gerald?"

Boone spun with a startled look on his face. Had he not heard me arrive or was he shocked by my question? Regardless, it garnered the response I was hoping for, so he could thank me later.

She sat up very straight suddenly, mouth a round "O" of horror, before she spoke. "No!" Melanie shook her head, thin, dark hair wavering around her hollow cheeks, deep circles making her red eyes look almost demonic. "I didn't hurt him, I swear. I wanted to, I'm not sorry he'd dead." She broke down into more tears, but these were bitter and angry, not stunned and blurred. "I went to see Trent, found the door to the bridal suite ajar. I thought he'd gone back in." Her hopes were clearly dashed. "Until I saw what had happened. It had to have been Gerald." She fumbled the tissues in her hands, dropping them to the floor, staring at them with hopeless eyes before meeting mine again. "I left," she said, now dull and drained of energy, falling back into the cushions. "I knew Trent would never want me again. I didn't want to kill Gerald anymore, Seph," she said. "I wanted to die."

I didn't get to respond to that, Carla snorting with derision.

"Don't be so dramatic," she snapped.

That was it. I couldn't take it anymore. The woman had to go down. Knowing I was tromping on Boone's very attractive toes but unable to restrain myself, I took a step past him and got in the woman's face. Eye-to-eye, I finally asked her the question I'd been dying to since Christmas Eve.

"At least she's not a traitor," I said. "Tell me, Carla, how long had you and Gerald been having an affair?"

The look on her face was far too satisfying for words.

CHAPTER NINETEEN

Boone might have been unhappy with me, but Melanie's reaction took the whole freaking cake. Carla's face turned unbelievably pale, shedding the redness of her rage in a rush of exiting blood pressure that had her falling back from me and half-turning to say something to the woman on the sofa. But Melanie was already up and throwing herself at Carla, her turn to shriek as she grabbed the former maid-of-honor by the hair and jerked her to the ground.

The detective scrambled to pull them apart, Melanie panting and fighting him, Carla crawling away from the attack, her turn to break into tears, though I doubted hers were anything but fed by bitter regret.

"Don't believe a thing this lying witch says!" Carla used a much harsher word to describe me, but I'll spare you the gory details. "I've been your friend your whole life!"

"I knew you were cheating with Gerald," Melanie screamed at her, "I just knew it! Seph would never lie to me. I can't believe you did this." The bride stilled, eyes bugging out as she spluttered a moment. "Did you trash the suite?" If Boone thought he had a wildcat in his arms previously, he had no idea. Melanie burst into renewed fury, trying to claw her way to the still retreating Carla who had dragged herself up from her hands and knees and cowered against the fireplace. "You (insert swearword here)!"

Melanie finally stopped fighting, though her cold, flat stare was almost worse than her rage. Carla, meanwhile, pulled herself together, though she quailed under the steady and deathly glare aimed in her direction.

"I have no idea what you mean," Carla panted.

"Liar." Melanie shook Boone off, the detective retreating to my side, but clearly at the ready to stop her again if necessary. There was a red mark on Carla's cheek that hadn't been there before so Melanie must have landed a blow. Not that I cared. In fact, if I'd been Boone, I would have let them battle it out. Instead, I waited with some impatience for Melanie to have her say. "I can't believe I trusted you again. I thought you were my *friend*." And here went the waterworks. Callie and Thalia hurried forward to support Melanie as Carla seemed to regain some of her original arrogance.

That was until Boone spoke up.

"We have evidence of your relationship with Mr. Berman," he said, not even trying for that calm and caring confidence I was used to, going right for flat accusation. Carla didn't comment when he went on. "And we're also aware of your visit to the suite last night and your participation in the mess left there." He waited for her to say something, holding onto the sequins found in the hot tub. As tempting as it was to push her harder, I leaned back and gave him his space because there was lots of time to nail her smarmy butt to the wall. My Christmas present to him. "Denying it won't stop the inevitable, Ms. Helland."

"Fine, whatever," she snarled, cutting the air with the flat of one hand, leaning into the mantle for support but all her vitriol surfacing at last, showing the truth of her feelings for Melanie in one sharp, hateful look. "I helped Gerald, sure." She tossed her dark hair, chunky highlights fuzzy from the fight, a mascara smear on her cheekbone and most of her blush gone on that side from contact with Melanie's hand. She looked like a half-made mannequin or would have if she didn't radiate such hate. "I got you drunk after the wedding," she sneered when she said that, "then came up to the suite and had a drink with Gerald. We trashed the place." She shrugged like it was no big deal. "Even had sex on your bed after. He was very appreciative." Her lewd gesture in Melanie's direction had the weeping woman snarling and regaining control of herself. Nothing like fury to squash hurt for a while. "I took a lot of joy in it,"

Carla hissed at her, "more than you'll ever know."

"Why?" Melanie's demand would have been more powerful if there wasn't a faint wail in her tone. "I don't understand."

"You never did," Carla shot back. "Gerald was *mine* until you came along." Melanie's face stiffened, head shaking slowly back and forth. "He took one look at you and your money and decided he'd rather be rich than happy. I convinced him he could be *both*."

"You could have had him," Melanie said, sagging into the sofa again. "I never wanted him."

That only seemed to infuriate Carla more as the other woman staggered toward her, jabbing an index finger at the now defeated Melanie who leaned into my daughter for support.

"You *never* deserved him," she spit.

"Oh, you clearly deserved one another." I interrupted on purpose because I was tired of watching Carla crush Melanie under her heel. The former bestie spun on me with another snarl, but I wasn't some sobbing, broken victim, oh no. She had no idea how much I was looking forward to taking her down.

"Stay out of this," Carla said.

"You and Gerald had your fun," I went on. "Then what? You had a fight? Over money, no doubt. I bet he was cutting you out of the fortune he was about to extort from Melanie, didn't he?" There was a flicker of a flinch, enough that I knew I'd pushed the right button, at least. "So, you pushed him into the hot tub and drowned him in it." Carla spluttered while I held one hand up. "Whose key did you use to go into the suite?"

Carla didn't comment. Thalia moved quicker than I did, than anyone, dumping out the small purse on the coffee table before Carla could stop her. Boone hissed something about illegal search and seizure, but I pointed at the keycard that had fallen to the glass and cocked my head at the furious woman.

"Let me guess," I said. "You've had Melanie's key this whole time." That had me turning to Boone whose scowl had only deepened. "One of the original pair, I believe, detective. And the last one, perhaps, to open the door to the suite before I found the body?"

He was going to kill me. I could see it in his eyes. Thank goodness for me, his phone hummed. Instead of murder, Boone chose to check his message. When he was done, he looked up again, that intent to strangle me now faded, offering up the phone. Despite his willingness to share, he still stiffened as I slipped in next to him to read the text.

Hey boss, the texter sent, labeled as Rachel Mutch, the forensics tech. *Got one more scrap off that cell from the tub*. While Boone deposited his phone in my hand, with a whispered, "how did you know?" before leaving me to approach Carla as I skimmed the message, marked as outgoing this time.

--golddigger, the text scrap read. *I don't need you anymore. Mel's money will keep me warm at night. See you around, C.*

I looked up as the detective's question penetrated

the fact that I had been right, and it was killing him.

"According to Mr. Berman's messages," he said, "he was cutting you off, Ms. Helland."

Carla's lips turned downward, chin dropping, malevolence embodied glaring at him from under her carefully shaped eyebrows. "I want a lawyer," she said.

"That's probably an excellent idea," Boone said.

CHAPTER TWENTY

His suggestion had the opposite effect, not silencing her at all but making her rage return. She, however, didn't require him to hold her back, though I preferred Melanie's thrashing fury to Carla's spiteful and hateful explosiveness.

"The bastard," she snarled. "After everything I did for him, he had the nerve to cut me off." She spluttered, eyes huge and spittle flying. "He dared kick me to the curb when I was the one who…" she trailed off, still breathing heavily, though finally seeming to realize her rant was putting her in the crosshairs of guilty party for one, please.

When she pulled herself back and together, her hands were trembling and her cunning had returned, just barely hidden beneath a veneer of civility that I trusted as much as I trusted her.

"Gerald made me help," she said, "with the mess." Sure, he did. "Things went exactly as I suggested."

"The first time you were there," Boone said. "What about the ten-minute visit at 10:30PM?"

She shrugged. "He'd texted me, told me he was no longer interested in our arrangement." That came out in a snarl as her surface tension cracked enough to show the viciousness beneath, but she managed to rein it in again. "After I'd slept with him, the…" She cleared her throat. "He said he changed his mind. So, I went to see him and have a conversation about how displeased I was." Her expression took on a chilly mask that quickly faded when she realized what she'd said. "But he wasn't there, I swear. He was already gone."

"Of course, he was," Boone said. "Except, he wasn't, Ms. Helland. He died in the hot tub. With a handful of white sequins."

She gaped at him, shaking her head. "No," she said. "I didn't kill him. Mel, I swear." Right, like any of us believed a word she said at this point. "Look, I heard Trent and hid in my room, saw him go in and come out again," she said. "Then that meddling old woman, Stella Gannister and her bodyguard poked around. I lifted Mel's key from her, yes, used that earlier in the night. But I was in my room. You saw me." She jabbed her finger at me. "I heard you coming to the door." She was practically begging me to agree.

"But Melanie was in the suite," I said. I'd seen

127

her sleeping on the sofa with her back to me. Hadn't I?

"Just her dress," Carla said. Wow, I'd been really tired, I guess, assumed the thing draped over the pile of pillows had been Melanie. "I hid in my suite until I heard you leave then went back inside, but Gerald was gone. I looked for him, but he was nowhere so I left. Went back to the bar and got Mel, brought her here. That's all I know until I heard the cops arrive." She seemed desperate now. "I'm telling the truth. All of it. He was drunk, so drunk. And he told me Stella was paying him off!" She was clearly reaching for things to save her now, even as Boone reached for his cuffs at the back of his jeans and headed toward her.

"You're really going to need that lawyer, Ms. Helland," he said.

"What do you mean, Grandmother was paying him off?" That caught Melanie's attention, at least. And not in a good way.

Carla's bitterness returned and she jerked against the cuffs but didn't fight too hard. "He was going to drop the lawsuit," she said, "because the Gannisters were paying him to go away. Nice family you got there, Mel."

"How did you wipe the security footage?" That was the only question I had remaining. I already had her locked up for life for murder and hoped she rotted in prison forever.

Her surprise and confusion were the only bitter aftertaste left as Boone led her to the door.

"I have no idea what you're talking about," Carla

said, and I believed her this time as she again protested, "I'm innocent! I didn't kill Gerald!"

The frustrating part? We'd won, the killer was caught, and I knew in my cruel little heart we had the right person. So, why then did a seed of doubt burst into life and prod me to ask—did we, though?

Did we?

CHAPTER TWENTY-ONE

Boone returned, the girls still comforting Melanie, while I met his green eyes with my own troubled ones.

"Don't tell me," he said. "Seph, she's guilty." He seemed convinced and he was the professional here. So, why wasn't I?

"I think we need to talk to Stella Gannister." I caught him before he could protest, my hand on his arm. "I realize you're far from done," I said. "You're too good of a detective to not make sure everything is in order. I'm just saying, before Stella barricades herself behind a wall of lawyers, you might want one more run at her."

He shrugged. "You seem to have her ear," he said, glancing at Melanie and keeping his voice down.

"I take it you want to do all the talking."

"There's no way Carla had the means to erase that footage," I said, recalling her social media and her education listed as liberal arts in college. "Unless she's hiding a background I didn't see, which, I admit, is possible." He was nodding. "That means she might have had help."

"All right," Boone said. "If we could link the Gannisters into the murder, that wouldn't be the worst outcome," he said. "I know your FBI friend would be delighted, considering his connection to their current surveillance." He meant Angelo Flores. "Should we loop him in?"

"I think we'd be better off keeping this family if we want Stella to cooperate," I said. I looked over my shoulder at Melanie. "The therapist in me hates to be manipulative, but it's much more likely Stella will talk if she's trying to convince Melanie to rejoin the family, don't you think?"

Boone's frustration had turned to faint shock and admiration. "You should have been a cop," he said. "You're way too good at this." I wasn't sure that was a compliment, however, since I now got to worry about my personal relationship with him. Did my cleverness as an investigator make him wary of trusting me?

Something to talk about at another time. Right now, I had my conscience to absolve.

Trent was easy to corral thanks to Cherise and had sobered up sufficiently he was at least coherent and no longer a disaster, though he hadn't showered or shaved and looked nothing like the precise and put together FBI agent I was accustomed to. So weird to see him tipsy and out of sorts and it wasn't even noon. Melanie seemed as shocked to see him that way as I had been and immediately rose when he entered, though she stayed where she was and allowed him to come to her.

Which he did, to my relief. There was a long, aching stretch of quiet between them where the rest of us might as well have been on the moon before Trent embraced her and she clung to him with a low cry of relief.

Stella and Domino joined us a moment later, escorted by an officer, and it was no surprise to find Brin with them. The old woman took a seat without preamble, Brin perching next to her either out of newfound loyalty or a message to her mother (or both), though Melanie seemed so relieved by Trent's relenting, sitting next to her and holding her hand, she didn't appear as upset by Brin's camp choice as she probably would have under other circumstances.

Boone stood back, leaning into the fireplace, while I turned to Stella, faint nervousness at having the detective observing me so closely banished with irritation at being so silly. I dug deep into my therapy training and did my best show of compassion to the gathering before speaking.

"Carla Helland has been arrested," I said. Trent seemed surprised, then sad, hugging Melanie, Brin's scowl at her mother almost like blame. Had Melanie's daughter spoken up about the ex-friend? Likely, though that didn't matter now. "However," I said, "the security camera footage from this floor was erased rather precisely, making it harder for the detective to prove his case." I kept all blame out of my voice, only allowing regret.

To my surprise, Stella nodded. "While I'll deny it on the record," she said, "I may have suggested strongly to the night manager that his Christmas bonus could be easily doubled if such footage were to accidentally meet such a fate." Her steady expression held no guilt, though she did incline her head to Boone. Even as I considered his absence from the desk prior to my arrival and request for a key to the bridal suite. Was he up to no good at that moment? Surely, he'd have the wherewithal to erase said footage as Stella suggested. At least that satisfied one part of my curiosity. "It was never my intent to impede your investigation."

"Only to protect your family," I said. "You were concerned Melanie did it."

The bride stared in mute sorrow at her grandmother who sighed deeply.

"I did," she said. "Forgive me, my dear."

"You also paid off Gerald Berman," I said. "Isn't that right?"

Stella shrugged with great dignity, chin up. "He was being a nuisance," she said. "I made him go away." Again with the nod to Boone. "Without killing him." She focused on the couple on the sofa. "I only wanted my granddaughter to be happy and have the wedding and happy life she dreamed of. While Gerald's presence interfered with the first, I could, at least, assist in the second by means I have in more than sufficient quantity."

Melanie seemed stunned by the revelation, but Trent more so. "I'm an FBI agent," he said, like that was a huge revelation to everyone or something.

"You don't say," Stella said so deadpan I snorted.

"You can't just..." Trent trailed off, sagging back into the cushions, gaze lost in the distance.

"This is why I didn't tell you," Melanie said very softly to the man she obviously loved, voice heavy with regret. "I should have, Trent. I'm so sorry. But I honestly thought I had put the family behind me. Grandmother agreed to let me go. This should never have been an issue." Anger rose again as she faced off with Stella.

But the matriarch of the Gannister family didn't relent. "I *did* let you go," she said. "I have never once interfered in your life, even when you lost our dear Evan." Melanie flinched at the mention of her departed son, but Stella carried on regardless. "I didn't even request to meet Brin." The young woman's hand tightened on her great-grandmother's. "All I wanted was to attend your wedding. A wedding, I must say, I'm glad I crashed regardless of your desires, considering. I only wish I had known of Gerald's plan before he ruined your happiness."

I believed her and, apparently, so did Brin.

"This isn't Great-Grandmother's fault, Mom," she said. "You're the one who did all the lying and deceiving." She seemed greatly offended by that.

"Why did you send Domino to investigate the suite?" I shifted interest to Stella who had an answer

134

at the ready.

"It was my intent to ensure Gerald left the premises," the old woman said. "By the collar of his jacket, if necessary." She grimaced as she shifted positions as though her old body was giving her trouble, though I doubted very much she was in real discomfort, using her age as a weapon yet again. "However, Domino's search failed to turn up that bad penny despite my assumption Gerald had something to do with the destruction of the bridal suite." She met Trent's eyes with her own. "I've already taken care of the damages," she said. "Welcome to the family, Trent dear."

Yikes. The implication that her manservant would have done the deed if Domino found Gerald in the suite wasn't lost on me, though it only assured me Stella and her manservant had nothing to do with the man's death. Why admit to something if her bodyguard for hire was actually guilty?

His disappointment showed on Domino's face, only reassuring me neither of them had anything to do with Gerald's murder. As for Trent, I felt sorry for him. He had no idea what he'd actually signed up for, not like him, either. Love made us all idiots, it seemed.

Melanie couldn't argue either, could she? "I made a mess of all of this," she said to her daughter, and to Trent. "Can you forgive me?"

Brin looked away, arms crossed over her chest, but Trent appeared to be helpless to her request no matter how uncomfortable the situation.

"Of course," he said, cuddling her close to him,

seemingly in a daze. The FBI agent couldn't resist, to my shock, and caved despite himself. "I love you."

"I love you, too." Melanie's crying started up again while Stella turned to me.

"Perhaps a moment of family time," the old woman said. Not a suggestion, though she couched it as such. Domino moved immediately toward the door, opening it for me. Boone joined me, Cherise on our heels, my girls mute and subdued as they exited together. The door closed firmly behind us, though Boone left an officer outside the door.

"I'm family," Calliope said, bitterness making me hug her to me.

"You are," I whispered in her ear. "*My* family. I love you more than anything."

She squeezed me tight. "Thanks, Mom." She and Thalia left, arms around one another, disappearing into our suite while Cherise sighed.

"Trent's got a mess on his hands with that bunch." She squinted at Boone. "You going to push the Gannister investigation?"

"There's time for that later," he said. "I'll have a chat with Agent Flores before this is over."

She seemed confident in that decision. "Well, maybe we can all get back to our vacation now." Cherise shook Boone's hand before hugging me and then returning to her own suite, closing the door behind her.

I looked up at the detective who was frowning at the floor, hands on his hips, light catching that obnoxious "B" he wore front and center. I'd always meant to ask him about it and never did, since he didn't come across as the flashy type to me, but before I could ask, he broke out of his reverie and met my eyes.

"I have to go back to work," he said. "There's a ton of paperwork to do and an official interrogation once Carla Helland has a lawyer present." His regret mirrored my own.

"Of course," I said, doing my best not to show him how much I wished he could stay. If I learned anything about being in a relationship with someone in law enforcement, it was that they put their jobs first, always. Then again, I did too, right? So, it was only fair.

Boone leaned in, pressing his lips to my forehead. "I'll call you." I watched him turn and go, heading for the elevators, leaving me with a mix of emotions I wasn't sure I could unpack.

CHAPTER TWENTY-TWO

I couldn't go back to my suite. My mind was just too active and despite running on little sleep, I found myself again prowling the hotel in search of my cat. Despite the fact the case was over, I couldn't shake the feeling something wasn't right and, as I headed outside for a quick peek in the garden my suite overlooked, I found myself frowning at the ground.

It took longer than it should have for me to register the small footprints marring the snow lining the walk thanks to my busy brain but, when I finally did, I gasped out loud. They had to be fresh, too, those Bella-sized prints, because we'd had snow only a few hours ago and I'd walked this space before with no luck.

"Bella!" I called her name, making the requisite

138

psss psss psss sound to summon her, trembling as I stood very still to listen.

And heard her cry, soft and plaintive, coming from further down the path.

I was not dressed for snow, my slippers sliding over the skiff of white stuff on the paving stones, my sweater barely enough to ward off the chill, but none of that mattered as I slipped and slid my way to the end of the enclosed garden, fighting panic and anxiety and the need to go slowly so I didn't scare her off again.

"Bella!" I spotted her crouched under a bush in the far corner of the garden, lunging for her despite knowing moving slowly was a better choice. Except it was clear to me my cat had enough of her little adventure because when I reached for her, she leaped at me, practically wrapping her furry forelegs around my neck and bursting into purrs between meows of delight as if to say, "I've been looking everywhere for you, silly! Where have you been?"

I cradled her and let myself cry into her fur, all the stress of missing her dissipating as she snuggled closer. "Bella," I finally choked in a thickened whisper, "you silly, silly cat. Don't ever scare me like that again."

She muttered something that wasn't a promise, I was sure, but seemed utterly content to be in my arms. I turned to head back inside, looking up and realizing I was right under the bridal suite balcony.

Even as my gaze took in what looked like a footprint on the wall beneath it.

That was weird. How could anyone leave a dirty

footprint flat on a wall like that? My gaze fell to the ground beneath it and the depression in the flowerbed that had been tilled for winter, snow covering the impression but leaving behind just the hint of where a shoe had settled into the as-yet unfrozen dirt.

As a horrible feeling settled in my stomach.

I balanced Belladonna in my arms while I whipped out my phone and sent a quick text, chest tight, pulse pounding in my ears, the cat still purring heavily enough it almost drowned out my heartbeat. It only took a moment to receive a reply, the sender's honesty surprising but telling me what I needed to know. Groaning in understanding, I fired off a text to Boone. The cold had finally gotten through to me, shivering making it hard to thumb-type and hold Bella, so I turned to go inside and finish what I'd started, making it to the door and into the hallway, head down over my phone as I hurriedly penned a group message to Cherise and Trent.

I didn't get to hit send. Someone grabbed me from behind and jerked on me, Bella clinging to me with her claws as she yowled a warning, but too late. I stumbled through the open doorway and felt myself almost fall as I was spun and pushed forward, catching myself just before I fell to my knees. My cold hand spasmed as I did, phone falling to the floor with a thud, text on the screen facing up, ready to be sent.

Shaking from cold and adrenaline, I turned to find Angelo Flores had closed the door behind us, the empty suite quiet and dark, just enough light coming through the windows to catch the white rectangle of a master key in his grip. Oh, and don't forget the glint of the gun in his other hand.

All of which I processed in about a half second as he spoke.

"I really wish you'd stopped digging," he said.

CHAPTER TWENTY-THREE

Bella hissed at Angelo, ears flat back, fangs showing. He ignored her while I held her close, not wanting to give him any reason to hurt her, though his intent was clear, wasn't it?

"I didn't want to have to kill you," he said. Yup, clear enough. "But you gave me no choice."

"Carla's in custody," I said. "Who are you going to blame my death on, Angelo?" Boone had to have gotten the text I sent, right? Though I hadn't had time to hit send on the one to Cherise and Trent. For all I knew, Boone was too far away to save me, but at least he'd be able to arrest Angelo. Fat lot of good that meant for my survival chances.

Selfish at a time like that? You better believe it.

"I have time," he said. "They'll find you in the

snow, blow to the head. They'll think you slipped and fell, out looking for your cat." He motioned at the patio doors behind me. "A shame, but accidents happen."

"Like killing Gerald was an accident?" I started backing up when he motioned for me to do so but moved slowly. I had to buy some time. My foot kicked my phone, spinning it further away from me, so no help there. Boone was my only chance.

"I know about your real deal with the Gannisters," I said. "Stella confirmed it." That surprising admission had come with her favorite caveat, *Hypothetically, you understand.* "Gerald wasn't your CI. He was your connection to the family."

"I screwed up ten years ago," Angelo said, relentless forward motion shoving me backward, my awkward circling of furniture taking me close to the balcony doors. For a brief instant I had the sofa between us, but Angelo was faster than me, and his gun hand unwavering, so by the time he spoke again, his access was again unfettered, and I was close enough to the glass I could feel the cold radiating through it. "Gerald and the Gannisters made it go away." He shrugged. "Not all of us are Trent Garret," he said with what sounded like regret. "I had debts I owed to very bad people. And the bribe was just too rich to resist."

"The arrest and conviction of Hylan Gannister was part of it," I said.

"The family wanted him gone," Angelo agreed. "He was a problem, so they set him up to take the fall and gave me an alibi for everything else. I've been

143

in charge of the investigation against them ever since."

"A win-win," I said. "Until you left the division."

Angelo snarled at that. "I wasn't given a choice."

"Stella didn't know that," I said. "That's why she was so eager to betray you, Angelo." I didn't know why, not officially, she'd answered my hasty text with honesty. "She told me what you did." That much was true, at least, however. Stella's motives remained her own.

"She's been looking for the means to cut me off," he said. "I guess I've been asking for too much." Did she have some connection in the FBI that got him transferred? A question for another time, though greed was an excellent motive to kick him to the curb.

"You could do a lot of damage to the family," I said. What was Stella's game? She had to have information that would assure her family's safety or there was no way she would have given me what I needed.

"She knows I'll never talk," Angelo said. "I took care of Gerald. She owes me." Wait, Stella asked him to kill Gerald? But the FBI agent shook his head as though he read my mind. "I haven't worked for them since I was pulled, after Hylan's conviction. Outside of keeping the investigation from turning up anything. As much as I'd like to blame her, Gerald's death is all me." He laughed then, bitter and angry. "Stella cut him off years ago, when Melanie left. Gerald approached me before the wedding, was going to report me if I didn't help him blackmail

Stella. I honestly didn't know he was going to ruin Trent's wedding." Angelo seemed oddly sad about that. "Or I would have killed him sooner."

"You set Carla up to take the fall," I said as he gestured for me to open the door behind me. I reached for the handle, knowing if I went out on that balcony there would be no saving me, but not sure what else to do.

"I was in the suite when she and Gerald were trashing the place," he said. "But as soon as she left, I took care of business."

"You scaled the wall," I said.

He sighed deeply. "How did you know?"

"You left a footprint," I said.

Angelo shook his head. "I should have checked." He stared down at the floor, hand unwavering but frowning and expression distant. "Too many balls in the air. I'm getting soft." He shrugged then, meeting my eyes, his dead and cold. "No matter. I'll take care of it when I find your body."

Yeah, no thanks. "You saw him fight with Carla." Come on, Boone. My phone lit up behind Angelo, a text landing, but he didn't see it. Hope surfaced, even if it was only a flicker of it, giving me the courage to drop my hand and press my back to the door, refusing to go outside as I challenged Angelo.

His jaw jumped, expression flattening out further. "Outside, now."

"Make me." I held on as he seemed to debate just shooting me before he spoke again.

"I watched them fight," he agreed. "When she left, I lured Gerald to the balcony and drowned him in the tub with one hand. I knew if anyone saw my sleeve it would be wet, so I dumped champagne over it."

"And you gathered sequins and put them in the tub to make Carla look guilty." Smart, very smart.

"Too many balls in the air," he repeated. "Damned soft dirt." He reached toward me with his free hand, gun pressing into my stomach as he slid the door open behind me. "When I heard others had visited the room after me, I assumed I'd gotten away with it. Carla was the perfect suspect, after all, and obliged me with her second visit. She's guilty of many things, Seph, so she can go down for murder for all I care." He paused briefly before refocusing. "There, you have your story," he said. "Now, let's get this over with."

There was nothing I could do, even when he backed up a half-step, gun no longer in contact. He was at such close range, finger on the trigger, if I fought him, I'd die.

Bella didn't know that, though. Whatever passed through her furry head, she had no clue I was in mortal danger from the weapon pointed at me. All she knew, I could guess, was that I was unhappy and the tall man before us was the one making me squeeze her so hard.

She lashed out with both front paws, claws hooking in his cheek, raking his face with her fury. Both of Angelo's arms rose to ward her off in an instinctive gesture, the gun going off, the sound so close to my ears my head rang from the concussive force. Adrenaline surged, my cat leaping from my arms as I tackled the FBI agent who was already off balance from Bella's surprise attack. He stumbled backward, landing hard against the sofa as the door to the room burst open, Angelo hitting the floor, his gun spinning away as I collapsed on top of him.

Boone's arms never felt so good as he lifted me free of the dazed murderer, Trent and Cherise taking their friend in custody while Belladonna perched on the back of the sofa, grooming his blood from her claws and looking quite pleased with herself.

CHAPTER TWENTY-FOUR

The toasty fire hummed happily in the fireplace, warm blanket wrapped around me almost too hot, though I'd fight anyone who tried to take it from me. I flipped the page on my book, sipping a delicious glass of gin while my cat purred softly on the edge of sleep, curled into a ball on my stomach.

The girls had left to go skiing a couple of hours earlier, our decision to extend our vacation by a few days last minute but welcome. Thanks to an offer from the overwhelmed and still gracious general manager, Kate Nimitz, we had our suites for free for two more nights. It wasn't her fault her day manager, Yuri Ellsworth, had decided to pad his salary, though I did hear he'd been fired while the Maine State Police wanted a word with him. That would teach him to tamper with evidence in a murder investigation.

As for the young maid, I'd put in a good word with Ms. Nimitz and was rewarded with a big hug from Cyndi Milo, along with profusive promises to watch for Bella every time she came near the room.

My cat's return had been greeted with many pats, kisses and treats, the ridiculous creature making no effort whatsoever to move much past my bedroom or the living room sofa since she saved my life. Whatever adventure she'd gotten up to in the two days she'd been missing, she wasn't saying, though I was indeed happy she was not only safe but had been with me to save the day.

She didn't know it yet, but I'd be fitting her with a GPS collar the moment we arrived home and she'd be the queen of her own tracking app shortly thereafter.

With Angelo Flores in custody and Carla Helland released, I'd said a grateful farewell to Stella Gannister that morning, Domino hovering near her car door, Brin holding her great-grandmother's hand.

"Mr. Flores outstayed his usefulness," Stella told me. "And while he may think he has information he can trade about my family, please assure the FBI and Detective Boone the Gannisters welcome any inquiry he may consider pertinent." Which meant she'd likely been playing him all along and whatever Angelo thought he had was useless.

The fact I'd seen her talking with Thalia earlier that morning factored into it. But when I asked what they'd discussed, Stella told me in no uncertain terms to mind my own business.

"The child has a weight to bear," she said. "I merely offered advice, one heiress to another." Hopefully not illegal, but whatever. "You are an excellent influence," Stella told me then, squeezing my hand. "She's lucky to have you, dear Persephone. I do hope I, too, can benefit from your presence from time to time."

I found myself hugging Stella and admiring her cleverness and grace, though I was certain she and her family had crimes to answer for. Murder, however? I didn't think was one of them, so I'd be leaving the investigation up to the proper authorities.

I was sad for Melanie, in a way, Brin hugging me briefly before leaving with Stella. Though, when I helped her ready herself for the second attempt at wedded bliss last night, the small ceremony she and Trent hastily put together requiring assistance to pull off, she didn't seem so upset as all that.

"Brin has the right to make her own choices," Melanie said. "And so do I."

That's how I found myself, along with Cherise, standing as witness to the wedding of my ex-husband to his new bride, as weird as that sounds. Whatever Trent told himself to justify marrying Melanie, he'd clearly come to personal terms with aligning himself with the Gannisters, though I wasn't sure how well his bosses would take the revelation.

That was on my ex. He chose love over work and that made me prouder of him than he'd ever know.

The sheriff and her husband had left for home

this morning, leaving Layla to ski with the girls. I'd given over my room in the suite to the younger King when another offer had been made and was more than happy with my decision for some privacy.

Especially when tall, dark and handsome joined me on the sofa, Belladonna protesting softly as Kellan Boone slid in beside me and rested his head on my shoulder. Callie hadn't commented on the fact the detective lingered or that I'd moved out of our suite to take up habitation in his. We'd be having a conversation about my dating choices, I had no doubt, but for now, either Thalia kept Calliope from giving me a hard time or my kid decided even I deserved a bit of happiness, thanks.

Whatever the reason, I was determined to make the most of what was left of my holiday and wanted Boone in it.

I set aside my book, arms around him and my cat, the soft crackle of the fire soothing as the scent of him was as delicious as it was enticing.

"You said something about a present," I blurted as the thought flashed in my mind from nowhere. Whatever our headbutting over the case, he'd been good enough to let it go and I'd chosen to do the same. But the mystery of his suggestion I enjoy his gift surfaced and I couldn't let it go.

He chuckled and sat up, arms out, grinning. "Merry Christmas," he said. And waited for me to get the punchline.

Which I did, believe you me, in a tantalizing shiver of anticipation. I laughed, leaning forward, disturbing my cat who grumbled as she hopped down and curled up on the carpet in front of the fire.

Because he was the perfect gift, really, and our chosen activity to celebrate his present didn't leave room for her, anyway.

Looking for the next Persephone Pringle mystery? Book nine, *Blast from the Passed*, is coming soon!

PERSEPHONE PRINGLE COZY MYSTERIES: NINE

BLAST FROM THE PASSED

WELCOME

PATTI LARSEN

ABOUT THE AUTHOR

Everything you need to know about me is in this one statement: I've wanted to be a writer since I was a little girl, and now I'm doing it. How cool is that, being able to follow your dream and make it reality? I've tried everything from university to college, graduating the second with a journalism diploma (I sucked at telling real stories), am an enthusiastic member of an all-girl improv troupe (if you've never tried it, I highly recommend making things up as you go along as often as possible) and I get to teach and perform with an amazing group of women I adore. I've even been in a Celtic girl band (some of our stuff is on YouTube!) and was an independent filmmaker (go check out the Lovely Witches Club). My life has been one creative thing after another—all leading me here, to writing books for a living.

Now with multiple series in happy publication, I live on beautiful and magical Prince Edward Island (I know you've heard of Anne of Green Gables) with my multitude of pets.

I love-love-love hearing from you! You can reach me (and I promise I'll message back) at https://patti@pattilarsen.com. And if you're eager for your next dose of Patti Larsen books (usually about one release a month) come join my mailing list! All the best up and coming, giveaways, contests and, of course, my observations on the world (aren't you just dying to know what I think about everything?) all in one place: https://bit.ly/PattiLarsenEmail.

Last—but not least!—I hope you enjoyed what

you read! Your happiness is my happiness. And I'd love to hear just what you thought. A review where you found this book would mean the world to me— reviews feed writers more than you will ever know. So, loved it (or not so much), your honest review would make my day. Thank you!